"You May Have Seduced One DeLuca, But I'm Not As Easily Impressed As My Brother."

"I haven't been trying to impress you," she told him. "And what makes you think I would want to go round two with anyone with the last name DeLuca?" She stood and whirled away.

He snagged her wrist, pulling her against him. Her hand fell against his chest and she felt his heart against her palm.

"Hold on to that thought," he said. "You're going to need it. But just so you know, if you ever went to bed with me, you would never think of it as round two."

Dear Reader,

Have you ever made a doozy of a mistake? One that impacted you and perhaps others for months, maybe years to come? Most of us make mistakes every now and then—if not every day. But I wanted to write about a heroine who had made a doozy of a mistake by getting involved with and becoming pregnant by the wrong kind of guy. What I love about my heroine Lilli is that she decides to make the very best of the situation, and be the best mother possible.

What kind of man would be a match for her? I was inspired by the idea of writing about a man of steel with a deep sense of responsibility, but no heart. A billionaire who does not believe in romantic love, who guards his heart because the men in his family have a history of being ruined by scheming women who use them. Max DeLuca is determined never to be played the fool by a woman. So what happens when it looks like his worst nightmare has come true? Is it possible that the man of steel could actually have a heart of gold?

Enjoy the ride of this passionate story and stay tuned for more billionaires coming your way in the near future.

I wish you love…

Leanne Banks

LEANNE BANKS

BEDDED BY THE BILLIONAIRE

Silhouette® Desire

Published by Silhouette Books

America's Publisher of Contemporary Romance

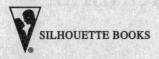

SILHOUETTE BOOKS

ISBN-13: 978-0-373-76863-9
ISBN-10:   0-373-76863-X

BEDDED BY THE BILLIONAIRE

Books by Leanne Banks

Silhouette Desire

Royal Dad #1400
Tall, Dark & Royal #1412
His Majesty, M.D. #1435
The Playboy & Plain Jane #1483
Princess in His Bed #1515
Between Duty and Desire #1599
Shocking the Senator #1621
Billionaire's Proposition #1699
†*Bedded by the Billionaire* #1863

*The Royal Dumonts
†The Billionaires Club

LEANNE BANKS

is a *New York Times* and *USA TODAY* bestselling author who is surprised every time she realizes how many books she has written. Leanne loves chocolate, the beach and new adventures. To name a few, Leanne has ridden on an elephant, stood on an ostrich egg (no, it didn't break), gone parasailing and indoor skydiving. Leanne loves writing romance because she believes in the power and magic of love. She lives in Virginia with her family and her four-and-a-half-pound Pomeranian named Bijou.

Special thanks to Cindy Gerard, Rhonda Pollero
and all my wonderful, supportive writing friends
and the great Melissa Jeglinski,
who continues to make my work better!

This book is dedicated to the comeback kid in all of us.

One

"I understand you're pregnant with my brother's child."

Lilli McCall instinctively put her hand over her swollen belly and studied Maximillian De Luca. She'd reluctantly allowed him and his associate into her small suburban Las Vegas apartment. Heaven knew, she'd had several unwelcome visitors since Tony De Luca had died two weeks ago.

She'd spotted the family resemblance between Tony and Max through the peephole of her door—the natural tanned complexion, similar bone structure. Only this man wasn't as pretty as Tony. Tony had been full of easy smiles and charm, and ultimately lies. This man's face was so hard she wondered if it would break into pieces if he smiled.

Tony had told her about his brother, Max. He'd frequently complained that his brother was cutthroat, even with his own family. He'd called him the man of steel, a steel mind and a steel heart.

Lilli had detached herself from Tony for good reasons. She wanted nothing to do with him, his friends or his family.

"Miss McCall?" Max prompted.

Taking a quick breath, she gave a slow nod, willing herself not to be intimidated by the tall man. "Yes, we got involved after my mother died, but things didn't work out between us," she said in a voice she knew was stilted, but she couldn't smooth it for the life of her.

"The details aren't necessary. As you know, my brother died in an automobile accident. He had no will and no provision for children, so—"

"I didn't expect anything from him," she interjected.

He paused, his gaze flickering over her in a considering way again. "Really," he said in a doubtful voice.

His tone jabbed at her. "Really," she said. "Tony was kind to me after my mother died, but it became clear to me that I didn't belong in his world."

"Why is that?"

"I—" She hesitated, her chest tightening as she remembered the fateful night that had made her break up with him for good. "We had different values. I wanted the baby brought up in a different environment."

His gaze fell to her pregnant belly. "You came to that decision a little late, didn't you?"

In more ways than he could know, she thought. "Yes, but I can focus on the baby or on my failures. Focusing on my failures isn't going to help me. So," she said, more than ready for him to leave, "since I wasn't expecting anything from Tony, you don't need to—"

"That's where we disagree," he said and nodded toward the man standing behind him. "Jim, could you give me the paperwork? Lilli, this is Jim Gregory. You may recognize him as someone who has knocked on your door a few times recently."

Lilli tore her gaze away from Max long enough to look at the older man and recognized him. "I apologize," she said. "I live by myself, so I'm not really comfortable opening the door to men I don't know."

"I understand," Jim said and she thought she saw a hint of compassion in the older man's eyes. "Here it is, Max," he said, producing some papers from a manila envelope, along with a pen.

Max took the papers and pen and handed them to Lilli. "It's a simple document. In exchange for one million dollars now and another million dollars if and when the child reaches the age of twenty-five, you agree to give up any rights to my brother's inheritance. If you should die or fail to raise the child in a responsible manner, you agree to relinquish custody of the child to a suitable guardian of my choice."

Lilli felt her jaw drop to the floor.

"It's all there," Max said. "Let me know if you have any questions."

Lilli stared blankly at the paper and felt her hands begin to shake with anger. Shoving the papers back at him, she stepped backward. "Are you nuts?"

"Should have known," Max said to Jim. "I told you she would want more money."

Stunned, Lilli continued to stare at him. "So you *are*

nuts," she said. "You didn't hear me earlier, did you? I didn't expect anything from Tony. I don't now. And I certainly don't expect anything from you. And if you think for one second that I would let someone I've never met choose who raises my child, you're totally crazy."

"That clause is just to protect the child in the event of your death or in case you develop any dangerous habits." He placed the agreement on top of her mother's marble-top table. "Read it. Sleep on it. I'll negotiate the amount within reason."

She snatched it up to give it back to him again.

He shook his head and held up his hand. "The drama is unnecessary. It costs a lot to raise a child. It will be difficult since you're doing it alone. Think about your child's needs. Do you really want to give up everything this money can buy for your child?" He paused while her heart pounded in her chest five beats. "I'll be in touch."

As soon as the two men left her apartment, Lilli flipped the dead bolt in place. Incensed and insulted, she paced into the den. Her pulse was racing in her ears, her nails digging into her palms as she clenched her hands together. Who in hell did he think he was, coming into her home and talking to her that way?

Granted, there were a few things that didn't put her in the best light, such as the fact that she'd even gotten involved with Tony in the first place, and the fact that she was unwed and pregnant. But everyone made mistakes. The solution was owning up to them and making the best of whatever choices have been made.

Although she hadn't intended to get pregnant by Tony, Lilli was determined to be the best mother she could be. Even with all the uncertainty and responsibility she was facing, from the moment she'd learned she was carrying a life inside her, she'd felt a little less lonely.

Lilli walked into the nursery she had begun to decorate and took a deep calming breath. She'd given the walls a fresh coat of paint and hung a puffy Noah's Ark wall hanging with removable animals. The crib was solid maple, and she'd already attached a mobile with friendly colorful butterflies and birds. With her next paycheck, she planned to buy soft crib sheets and blankets in blue for her little guy.

Pressing her hand to her belly again, she thought of Max De Luca. She'd never met a man like him. Arrogant, insulting, charm-free. At least to her. She couldn't deny, though, that in different circumstances he would have fascinated her. But lions had always fascinated her, too, and she knew better than to get into a den with one of them.

"That went well," Jim said in a wry voice as Max led the way to the black Ferrari.

Loosening his tie a fraction of an inch, Max unlocked the car and slid behind the steering wheel. Max preferred being in the driver's seat. It gave him the illusion of control. He slid into the leather seat. "Damn Tony for this," he said, even though his grief was still fresh. "He was going to be a father, for God's sake. You would think he could have at least provided for his child."

"You've been cleaning up his messes a long time," Jim said as Max sped out of the apartment complex. "Just curious. Did you have to be a total ass to her?"

Max had known Jim since he was a child and that was the only reason he allowed the older man to talk to him so bluntly. "She surprised me," he said, shifting into fourth as he turned onto the interstate. "I was expecting one of those showgirls he went through like cheap wine."

"I told you she's a pediatric dental hygienist."

"I figured that was her day job. She had to have another angle." He shook his head. "She looked almost wholesome. I mean, aside from the bump, she had a nice body as far as I could tell. Did you notice she was wearing bunny slippers?"

Jim laughed. "Hard to miss them."

"She wasn't wearing a speck of makeup. Her hair color didn't look like it came out of a bottle. She looked soft," he said, still trying to come to grips with his impression of Lilli McCall. "Real. Not Tony's type at all."

"She must have been his type for a while."

Max felt his chest tighten in a strange way. How had Tony lucked into her? A woman like that shouldn't have been abandoned. Not if his first instincts about her were correct. "Yeah. He got lucky."

Lilli was that irresistible combination of soft and sexy that every man craved. It was all too easy to wonder how that mouth of hers would feel all over a man's body.

He felt himself grow warm at the thought and shook his head. He'd never been attracted to one of his brother's women. Turning the AC on high, he directed the vent at his face.

"I really ticked her off with my offer," he said, his lips twitching in amusement. She'd looked as if she would have gladly ripped out his vocal cords. He'd found her reaction surprising and oddly attractive.

That didn't change the fact that everyone had their

price. Even a blond woman with pink cheeks, bee-stung lips and blue eyes that lit up like sparklers when she was angry. "She'll take the money," he said to Jim, shifting gear. "They all eventually do."

Max would clean up this mess. He had a lot of practice. Left to deal with his father's disastrous personal and financial choices, Max had worked nonstop during the past ten years to rebuild the family name and wealth.

His investments had delivered triple returns. The merger of Megalos Resorts with De Luca Inc. to form Megalos-De Luca Enterprises had sent the shares of his stock in the company skyrocketing. Determined to keep talent in the merged company, the new board paid the top performers eight-figure salaries.

Max's father may have been kicked off the board of the family company, but Max was determined that the next CEO would be a De Luca. Nothing would stop him. Especially not a feisty little blonde who happened to be carrying a De Luca baby in her belly.

The following evening, as she left the dental practice where she worked, Lilli winced as she flexed her fingers. Three-year-old Timmy Johnson just couldn't resist chewing on her index finger. Although she wore rubber gloves, they didn't always protect her from a chewing child.

She worked late three nights a week for two reasons. One, she earned a little more money working after five and two, she didn't really have anything else to do in the evenings. It wasn't as if she were a party animal. She'd left that brief period of her life way in the past.

Pulling her keys from her purse, she walked toward

her trusty four-year-old blue Toyota Corolla. Just as she neared her car, two men stepped in front of her. They both appeared to be in their twenties and they looked so much alike they could have been brothers.

"Lilli McCall?" one of them said.

The one man looked vaguely familiar, although she couldn't recall his name. One of Tony's friends? She tensed. "Why do you ask?" She backed away.

Both men took a step toward her. "We're hoping you can help us."

She bit her lip and took another step back. "I—uh." She cleared her throat. "How could I possibly help you?"

"We're here about Tony," one of the men said with a shrug. "He left some unpaid debts. We knew you two were close and we were hoping you could help us."

She shook her head. "I broke up with Tony a long time ago."

"Not before he knocked you up," the other guy cracked. "That baby's gotta be worth something to the De Luca family. Tony must have left you something."

"He didn't," she said, even though her throat was squeezing tight with fear. "Look at my car. It's four years old. I'm working as a dental hygienist. Do I look like someone who is loaded?"

The men frowned.

"Maybe you're hiding it."

Frustrated and afraid, she shook her head. "I'm not. Just leave me alone."

"It would be a lot easier to leave you alone if we got our money." One of the men pulled a card out of his pocket and walked toward her.

She wanted to run, but her feet seemed to grow roots into the pavement. The man pressed his card into her hand. "Call me if you find something. We'll check back in case you forget."

Her heart racing, she watched the two men leave and felt sick to her stomach. How much longer would they harass her? And how many more of Tony's so-called business acquaintances were going to show up at her door?

Taking a deep breath, she walked quickly to her car and got inside. Maybe she should move out of town. That could be expensive, though, and she'd like to keep the few friends she'd made over the last couple of months. The idea of being surrounded by strangers after she had her baby unsettled her.

She mulled over a dozen different options as she drove through a fast-food restaurant and ordered a milk shake. After she got home, she sipped on it and changed into a tank top that covered her pregnant belly and a pair of terry cloth shorts. Then to drown out her disturbing thoughts, she turned on the television to watch a rerun of her favorite medical drama.

Five minutes later, her doorbell sounded. She sighed, hoping it was her best friend Dee, off early from her second job as an aerobics instructor. The doorbell rang again before she could reach it. She looked through the peephole, but her porch light wasn't on. She could only make out the shadow of a man.

Fed up, she pounded on her side of the door. "Go away! I don't have Tony's money. I—"

"Miss McCall," a male voice cut in.

Lilli immediately recognized that voice. Mr. Steel, she'd named him. She bit her lip.

"Lilli," Max De Luca said again. "Can I come in?"

She glanced down at her outfit. It was far from swim-suit bare, but she knew she'd feel more comfortable wearing something else. Armor would work. "I'm not really dressed for visitors."

"This won't take long," he insisted.

Swallowing a groan, she opened the door. "I don't think we have anything else to—"

Max walked past her. He was dressed in a black suit that probably cost more than her car. Meeting him again, she could see why Tony had resented his older brother. Max was taller, his shoulders were broader, and he oozed enough confidence for a dozen men. Lilli suspected he was the type who would command any situation no matter how he was dressed. Despite the hard edges of his face, there was something sensual about the shape of his mouth. His thick black eyelashes gave his dark eyes a sexual cast.

If he were inclined, she would bet he could reduce a woman to melted butter with just a look. There was nothing boyish about him. He was all man and he would want a woman as tough and confident as he, a raving beauty. Lilli knew she would never make the cut.

Max stared at her, his dark eyes flashing. "Why do you keep talking about my brother and his money?"

She met his hot, hard gaze. "Since Tony died, some of his business acquaintances have been asking me to pay off his loans."

He frowned. "You? Why you?" His expression turned cynical. "Were you involved in some of his business dealings?"

"Absolutely not. I told you I stopped seeing Tony

over six months ago because I realized we didn't share the same values." She remembered that terrible last night and closed her eyes, trying to push it from her mind. "We were only together for about four months."

"Long enough for you to get pregnant," he said.

Offended by his tone, she glared at him. "Just in case you weren't paying attention in your high school biology class, it doesn't take four months to get pregnant. It takes one time. One slip." She shook her head. "Listen, I didn't ask you to show up at my home, insult me, offer me a big check and threaten to take my baby away if you don't approve of how I'm raising him."

"Him," he said. "So it's a boy."

"Yes," she said and felt her baby move inside her. Cradling her belly, she watched as Max's gaze raked over her from head to toe. After lingering on her breasts and legs, his eyes moved back up to her mouth. The intensity in his eyes made her feel as if she'd stayed out in the sun too long.

He finally lifted his gaze to hers. "How many men have come asking for money?"

"Five or six," she said. "They usually come in pairs. I stopped answering if I don't recognize who's ringing the doorbell."

"So this has happened, what three, four times?"

She bit her lip. "More like seven or eight," she admitted. "And two men showed up in the parking lot of my office after work tonight."

He paused one moment then nodded. "You shouldn't stay here by yourself any longer. You can come and stay at my house. I have ten bedrooms with staff and security."

Stunned, she stared at him. "Whoa, that's kind of

fast. Don't you think they'll stop coming around when they realize I really don't have anything to give them?"

"But you do," Max said. "You have a De Luca growing in your belly. Did any of them give you contact information?"

"One of the guys tonight gave me his card."

"Please get it for me," he said in a voice that was so polite and so calm it made her uneasy.

"Okay," she said and went into her bedroom to retrieve the card from her purse. She gave it to Max.

"I'll have Jim find out about this guy by morning." Max looked at her intently. "You got involved with a De Luca. We're a powerful family and there are people who resent us. There are people who want to hurt us. If you really care about the safety of your baby, then you need to come home with me."

She immediately shook her head. "I just met you. Why in the world would I leave my apartment to go to your home?"

"Because you'll be safe there," he said, impatience threading his voice. "Do you really trust that door against someone determined to get inside?"

Her mouth went dry at the image of an intruder, but she refused to be intimidated. "You're deliberately trying to scare me."

"No, I'm not," he said. "I'm merely protecting you and my nephew."

His words rocked her. He seemed to take the responsibility for granted, where Tony had been just the opposite. She shook her head. Could two brothers be so different? "How do I know you're not like him?" she had to ask.

His eyebrow creased in displeasure. "Like who? Tony?" He gave a harsh laugh. "I'm nothing like my brother. Or my father, for that matter."

She wondered what that meant, but from his expression, she suspected there was a world of history in his statement. A world she wasn't sure she wanted to know. She felt his shimmering impatience, but she resisted the pressure. "The only thing I know about you is what Tony told me."

Max gave a slow nod. "And that was?"

She bit her lip, reluctant to repeat the insults. "I'm not sure it's a good idea for me to—"

"Okay, then let me guess. Tony said I was heartless and unforgiving, straitlaced, boring, power-hungry and greedy."

She winced at his accuracy. "I'm not sure he used those words. He did refer to you as a man with a steel heart and steel mind. And he said you were ruthless."

"Ruthless," he said with a nod. "That was the other word I forgot. Not that far off the mark. I can be ruthless and I guard my heart and mind. I'm not distracted and I won't be tricked or deceived. But tell me, if I were completely cold and ruthless, why would I give a damn about you and your baby's safety?"

Good point, she thought, but the man still made her nervous.

"What do your instincts tell you about me?" he demanded.

She bit her lip again, and felt a flash of disappointment in herself. "My instincts got a little off-kilter after my mother died. I'm not sure how much I can trust them."

His expression was enigmatic. "Then you have a choice to make. You can either trust your door to those thugs who have been showing up and who aren't going away. Or you can trust me."

Two

"Dee," Lilli said. "This situation is crazy."

Max paused just inside the open sliding-glass door that led out to the patio, and watched Lilli as she paced and talked on her cell phone. After just one night in his home, she looked rattled and nervous. He couldn't remember a time when he'd had to work so hard to get a woman to stay overnight at his place, and this one hadn't even slept in his bed.

"Oh, it has to be temporary," she said. "It has to be."

He turned to walk away.

"It's clear that I don't belong here and I'm sure Max De Luca would be thrilled if I could disappear from the earth."

He stopped at the mention of his name, curious despite himself. Turning around, he watched her wavy hair bounce against her shoulders and her silver hoop earrings reflect the late-afternoon sunlight. She was wearing shorts that revealed her long, shapely legs, and he noticed her toenails were painted a vibrant pink. A silver chain wrapped around her ankle. She was an odd mix of feminine and practical. He didn't know why, but he'd liked the combination of strength and vulnerability he'd witnessed in her last night. She'd been determined not to be a pushover, but she'd also revealed her regret over her involvement with Tony. Although Max could name a million reasons, he wondered what had made Lilli decide to break up with his brother.

"How would I describe Max? Tony always called him a man of steel, but he didn't mean it as a compliment." She laughed. "Yes, he's disgustingly good-looking and completely lacking in charm." She sighed. "Maybe I just bring that out in him. Anyway, I can't imagine staying here. I can't imagine a baby living here, spitting up on carpets that probably cost twice what my car does. And speaking of my car, you would get a good laugh at how ridiculous it looks in the garage next to a Ferrari."

Max felt a twitch of humor at her colorful descriptions. Crossing his arms over his chest, he decided to listen to the rest of the conversation. She was providing him with more amusement than he'd had in a while.

"His wife? I don't even know if he has one. This house is huge. Maybe she hides in a different wing. Or maybe he keeps her chained to his bed to take care of his every *need and pleasure*," she said in an exaggerated voice. "Come to think of it, he's not wearing a ring and he doesn't really strike me as the kind to pin himself down to just one woman. Not that it's any of my business," she added. "I would move to the other side of the world except I hate the idea of going to a new place with a baby and not knowing anyone."

The honest desperation in her voice slid past his cynicism.

"I know I should be more brave about this. Maybe it's just hormones. And what happened when I was with Tony doesn't help."

Besides the obvious, what exactly had happened between Lilli and his brother? Max wondered, and he decided to make his presence known. Clearing his throat, he pushed the sliding-glass door farther open.

Giving a jerk of surprise, Lilli turned to look at him. "Uh, yeah I should go now. Dinner next Tuesday with the girls. I wouldn't miss it. Bye, Dee." She turned off the phone and lifted her chin defensively. "I, uh, didn't see you."

He nodded. "Was your room okay last night?"

"It's beautiful, of course," she said. "Your entire house is beautiful."

"The parts of it you've seen," he said, recalling what she'd said about his bedroom. He could practically see her mind whirling, wondering how much he'd heard. "It was too late for me to give you the complete tour last night. I should do that tonight."

"Oh, you don't have to—"

"I insist. The rumors about the dungeon are all false," he joked and watched her eyes widen. Swallowing a chuckle, he continued to meet her gaze. "And your bed? Did it work for you? Too soft? Too hard?" Last night the image of her in bed had bothered him. He'd wondered what kind of nightclothes she wore, if she ever slept naked.

"Oh, no. It was very nice, thank you." She cleared her throat. "I've been thinking about my living arrangements and—"

"So have I," he interjected. "If you're free for dinner, we can discuss it then."

She worked her mouth in surprise then shrugged. "I'm free."

"Okay, then we can eat on the terrace." He glanced at his watch. "Will you be hungry in an hour?"

"Sure," she said. "How do you dress for dinner?"

He allowed himself a leisurely gaze down her body. He wondered why she made something inside him itch. "Casual is fine. It will be just you and me."

Despite Max's insistence that dinner would be casual, Lilli changed from shorts into a periwinkle cotton baby-doll dress she hadn't worn in a while.

To bolster her confidence, she stepped into a pair of sandals with heels. She suspected she would need every bit of confidence she could muster when she told Max that she was returning to her apartment.

She walked downstairs through a hallway of marble and a living area that looked as if it had been taken out of a high-end decorator magazine. The sliding-glass door was open and Max stood, holding a glass of red wine, in front of a warming stove. With his back to her, she couldn't miss the V-shape of his broad shoulders and his narrow waist.

She felt a strange dip in her stomach at the sight of him and grabbed an extra breath. He must have heard her because he turned to face her. He was dressed in slacks and a white open-neck shirt that contrasted with his tanned skin. Moving beside a small table already set with plates and platters with sterling covers, he pulled out a chair for her.

"The chef prepared orange juice and seltzer for you. Is that okay?"

"Very nice," she said, surprised he'd known about the no-alcohol-during-pregnancy rule because he didn't seem to have any children of his own.

"My chef has prepared one of his specialties. He's excellent, so you should enjoy it."

A woman dressed in a uniform appeared from the sliding-glass doors. "May I serve you now, Mr. De Luca?" she asked.

"Yes, thank you, Ada," he said. "Lilli, this is my assistant housekeeper. She assists my chief housekeeper, Myrtle. Ada usually covers the 6:00 p.m. to 6:00 a.m. shift, so if you need anything after hours, feel free to ring her."

He had an assistant housekeeper? Lilli took another gulp of her drink, feeling more out of place than ever. "It's nice to meet you, Ada."

"My pleasure," Ada said with a smile and proceeded to serve the meal.

As soon as Ada left, Max turned to her and lifted his glass. "To a good meal and a meeting of the minds."

His gaze dipped to her décolletage and she felt a shocking awareness of him as a man. A strong, sexual man. Pushing the feeling aside, she took a deep breath and gave a determined smile. "It was very generous of you to invite me to stay here last night and tonight. I've given it some thought and I believe it will be best for me to move back to my apartment."

He shook his head. "I'm sorry. I can't allow that."

She blinked. "Allow?"

"I have some information that makes the choice clear, but I intended to tell you after our meal. I suspect you're concerned about staying here. You're probably afraid this setup isn't conducive for a baby."

She nodded. "Yes."

"Please go ahead and eat."

Lilli wanted to protest, but politeness compelled her to force down a forkful of the beef dish. The delicious taste momentarily distracted her and she took another bite. "Oh, you were right about your chef. This is amazing."

"You'll find I'm often right," he said. "I learned at an early age not to allow emotion to determine my choices."

"Why?" she asked, taking another bite.

"I watched my father spend half his fortune trying to keep his mistress happy."

She heard cynicism creep into his tone again, and for the first time understood why. "I'm assuming his mistress wasn't your mother," she ventured.

"She wasn't. She was Tony's mother."

"Oh," she said again, remembering something Tony had told her. "But I thought Tony's parents were dead."

"They are both dead. Died in a boating accident."

She set down her fork. "I'm so sorry."

He shrugged. "It was ironic because the boat was called Franco's Folly. My father's name was Franco. He spent a good part of his life chasing after things that eventually ruined him. Something I refuse to do. But that's a different subject." He took a sip of wine. "Jim did some research on the man who gave you his card yesterday. Trust me, he's bad news. You may as well be a sitting duck if you move back to your apartment without protection."

"Protection?" she echoed, appalled. "That's got to be an exaggeration. The man was a little pushy, but he backed off when I told him to. I'll just have to be very firm—"

"Lilli," Max interjected in a quiet, ultracalm voice that immediately got her attention. "It turns out he's involved with the local mafia. They're not above kidnapping or murder to collect on a debt."

Lilli froze, her appetite fleeing. "Oh, my God."

Nausea rose inside her and she turned from the table, automatically turning away. Terror coursed through her. How could she protect her child?

She felt Max just behind her. His body heat warmed her back. "You won't need to worry if you stay here. No one would dare hurt you as long as everyone knows you're in my care."

"Maybe I should go ahead and move out of town. I didn't want to do that, but—"

"You're too vulnerable for that right now," he said.

She turned to look at him. "What do you mean, too vulnerable?"

"Physically, for one thing. It's not like you'd be able to beat off an attacker."

"But if I moved away, I wouldn't have to beat off anyone."

He shook his head. "They're watching you too closely. Maybe later, but not now."

"Oh, God, I feel so stupid," she said, fighting back tears. "How did I let this get so out of control?"

"It could be worse," he said. "You can set up a nursery here. I'll cover the cost. We'll make the necessary adjustments in the house. Your life will be just like it was before, with a few perks."

"Just like before," she said, laughing with gallows humor. *As if anything could ever be like before.* "There's no way I could allow you to cover the cost of the nursery. It wouldn't be right. And I can't imagine living here. It's just so—"

"So what?"

"Perfect. This isn't at all what I pictured for my child."

"Why wouldn't my home be appropriate? I'm a blood relative. How is it right for your child not to know his uncle?"

Oh, Lord. She hadn't even thought of it that way. Her heart splintered. Her father had left before her third birthday and since her mother's relatives had lived on the other coast, she'd never had an opportunity to meet them, let alone enjoy any sort of family bond.

She shook her head. "I'd never considered any of this. Once I broke off with Tony, I knew it would be just me and the baby. I didn't think Tony's family would want to be involved, and frankly I didn't want anything to do with anyone bearing the name De Luca."

Max narrowed his eyes. "Tony and I are not the same man."

"I'm beginning to see that," she said. "I need to think about this."

"Finish your dinner," he said, cupping her arm with his strong hand. "We can discuss this more later."

Lilli's stomach jumped. She wasn't sure if it was a result of Max's hand on her bare arm or the terrible news he'd just delivered. She looked into his eyes and had the sense that this man could turn her world upside down in ways she'd never imagined. She stepped backward, needing air, needing to think. "I'm sorry, but I can't eat right now. Please excuse me. I need to go upstairs."

Max watched Lilli as she fled the patio through the door. With each passing moment, he felt more drawn to her, but for the life of him, he couldn't explain why.

Her immediate rejection of his offer to pay to furnish the nursery had caught him off guard. He was so accustomed to covering expenses for a multitude of people that he rarely gave it a second thought.

Women had always been more than happy to accept his generosity. In fact, on a couple of occasions, his companions had tried to take advantage of him. One woman had even gotten herself pregnant by another man and tried to make Max take responsibility for the child.

Lilli was the exact opposite. Unless it was all an act, which it could be, he thought, his natural cynicism rising inside him. Still, Lilli didn't strike him as a woman adept at hiding her emotions or motives.

He suspected she didn't want him to know that she was attracted to him, but he had seen it in her eyes. The attraction was reluctant, but strong, the same as it was for him.

In other circumstances, he would want her for himself. And he wouldn't just *want* her. He would take her.

Lilli paced her bedroom for two hours. With her head feeling as if it were going to split into a million pieces, she lay down and surprised herself by falling asleep. When she awakened at eleven-thirty, her stomach was growling like a mountain lion.

"Sorry, sweetie," she murmured, rubbing her stomach. The idea of that dinner going to waste nearly made her sob. Max had told her to call Ada, the housekeeper, if she needed anything, including a snack, but Lilli couldn't imagine imposing at this hour.

Dressed in a tank top and shorts, she quietly crept downstairs to the kitchen. She opened the refrigerator and peered inside. She found the leftovers and turned around.

"I'm glad you got back your appetite," Max said, startling her so much she almost dropped the container she was holding. Swearing under her breath, she managed to save the dish. Her heart racing, she backed away and closed the refrigerator door.

"I didn't think you would be down—" She broke off when she saw that he was shirtless, his pajama pants riding low on his waist. His chest was a work of art. Her mouth went dry.

"I heard a noise," he said casually, as if he didn't know that seeing him half-naked took her breath away.

She needed to keep it that way, she told herself and locked her gaze on his forehead. "I was hungry. I can just grab an apple and go back upstairs."

He moved closer to her and pulled the dish from her hands. "Why would you eat an apple when you can have this?" He put the dish in the microwave and started to warm it up.

Lilli tried very hard not to allow her gaze to dip across his naked shoulders, but she didn't quite succeed.

When the plate was hot, he directed her to a seat at the table.

Twenty minutes later, she'd polished off a reasonable portion of beef, bread and a brownie he'd insisted she eat.

She leaned back in her chair and stretched her legs. "That was delicious. Thanks."

His gaze enigmatic, he gave a slight smile. "You're welcome. Not bad for Mr. Steel."

Lilli blinked, then realized there was only one way he could have known she'd called him that. Her cheeks heated with embarrassment. "How long were you listening to my phone conversation?" she accused.

"It wasn't premeditated," he said. "I was going to tell you about the report I got from Jim, but you were so absorbed in your conversation that you didn't notice me."

Lilli closed her eyes, wishing she could hide. "Great."

"And no, I don't have a wife or mistress tied to my bed. I haven't found it necessary to tie women up to keep them in my bed."

She opened her eyes. "I didn't mean it the way—"

He waved his hand. "We may as well get this on the table. I know you're attracted to me," he said without a millimeter of arrogance.

She opened her mouth to deny it, but her throat closed around the lie.

"I'm flattered that you think I'm hot," he said. "But it's probably a good idea that you also think I'm cold because, for some reason, I find you attractive."

Lilli gaped at him, sure he was mocking her. "No."

"Yes," he said.

"But I'm pregnant," she blurted out. "And not with your baby."

"Your pregnancy doesn't conceal your other assets. It doesn't conceal your fire." His gaze traveled to her breasts and lower to her legs, then all the way back up to her mouth, making her feel as if a hot wind had blown over her. He gave a short laugh as if the joke was on him. "Don't worry. I'll get over it. You may have seduced one De Luca, but I'm not as easily impressed as my brother."

She felt as if he'd slapped her. "I haven't been trying to impress you," she told him. "Besides, your brother did the seducing, not me."

"It doesn't sound like you fought him."

"I didn't," she told him, but there'd been a time he'd taken advantage of her. "My mother died one week before I met Tony and I freely admit I was a mess." She met and held his gaze for a long, fierce moment. "And besides the fact that you're hot, what makes you think I would want to go round two with anyone with the last name De Luca?" She stood and whirled away.

He snagged her wrist, pulling her against him when she stumbled. Her hand fell against his chest and she felt his heart against her palm, his heat all over her.

"Hold on to that thought," he said. "You're going to need it. But just so you know, if you ever went to bed with me, you would never think of it as round two."

Looking into his hard, sensual gaze, Lilli felt a shiver run through her. Somehow, deep inside her, deeper than her bones, she knew that again he wasn't bragging. He was just telling the truth.

Three

Lilli awakened to the sound of the Bose alarm clock on the elegant bedside table. The strains of classical music lulled her into consciousness. Rolling to her side, she pulled the pillow over her head.

Just a couple more minutes. This bed was divine. It felt so wonderful she hated to leave it. Much better than her lumpy mattress back at her apartment.

She stiffened at the thought and immediately sat up in bed. Frowning, she told herself not to get used to this level of luxury. Sometime, more likely sooner than later, she would be living in a place where she was both the chief housekeeper and assistant housekeeper. There would be no Bose stereo systems and the closest she would get to a gourmet meal prepared by a chef would be a frozen dinner.

Rising from the bed, she padded across the luxury carpet to the large shower in the connecting bathroom. She would need to get up earlier since her commute to work was longer from Max's home. The very thought of him made something inside flutter and flip.

Hunger, she told herself. It had to be hunger or the baby. After she donned her colorful scrubs, she headed downstairs and was surprised to see Max pacing and speaking into a cell phone via a Bluetooth in his ear. He wore running shorts and a tank top that showed off his muscular legs and arms. Everything about him oozed strength. "Tell Alex we're limiting our domestic expansion until we see what happens with the dollar."

He saw her and lifted a hand. "Yes, I know Alex still resents that I was promoted over him. We each serve an important purpose. I provide the balance. He provides the fireworks. Tell him I said to think global. I'm working from home this morning. I'll be in the office this afternoon and will get an update then. Thanks. Bye."

He immediately turned to Lilli. "Good morning. Did you rest well?"

She nodded. "Yes, thank you."

"We have fresh-squeezed orange juice and the cook will be happy to prepare anything you like."

She shook her head. "I need to get on the road if I'm going to make it to work in time."

He frowned. "You can't skip breakfast. What about the baby?"

"I'll grab something at work. We always have fruit and bagels in the workroom," she said.

He shot her a disapproving glance. "That's not good nutrition."

"I don't think my baby is suffering. I'm taking my prenatal vitamins." He moved toward her and she struggled with the urge to flee. She was doing her best to keep her gaze fixed on his eyebrows. She refused to look into his eyes, or at his mouth, or at that stubborn chin or at those shoulders. Or lower. Feeling a flush of heat, she stepped backward. "Better go. See you la—"

"Your things from your apartment should be here by the time you return," he said.

Lilli stopped abruptly and blinked. "Excuse me?"

"I arranged for someone to pack your belongings and bring them here. Duplications like most of your furniture, dishes and linens will be put in storage. All the baby items will be moved into the nursery."

Trying to catch up with him, she shook her head in confusion. "Where is the nursery?"

"Across the hall from your bedroom," he said. "A decorator will be calling you later today so you can tell her what you would like done to it."

She shook her head again. "Did I ever actually say that I was going to stay here?"

He lifted a dark eyebrow. "There was another choice?"

She sighed, hating him for being right. "Well, you could have given me a little time to adjust to the idea. There's no reason I couldn't pack my own stuff and—"

His eyes widened in horror. "Moving in your condition?"

She sighed. "I'm very healthy. Women have been getting pregnant and delivering babies for years. In ancient times, it wasn't unusual for a woman to be

working in the fields one minute, having her baby the
next, then back at work immediately."

"I won't have you in the fields, period," he said in
a dry tone. "In terms of the speed of the movers, there
was no need to wait. We both agree, even if you don't
want to admit it, that you belong here until we figure
out a safe place for you and the baby. And that will be
months from now."

She made a face at his imperious tone. Lord help her,
he sounded like an emperor.

"In the meantime, I've asked my personal attorney
to draw up some documents regarding custody of the
child in case something should happen to you."

Lilli felt a chill. "I already told you I'm not signing
those papers. If signing those papers is part of the bar-
gain for me staying here, then I'm leaving."

"I never said that."

"No, but even you admitted that you could be ruthless. I'm not signing my child over to Ruthless Mr.
Steel," she said, mentally drawing a line and daring
him to cross over it.

"Yet," he said.

"I won't be manipulated over this," she warned him.

"Manipulation is for sissies," he said with a scoff.

"Then what do you call what you do?" she asked.
"Bullying?"

"Reason and logic prevail among rational human
beings."

Lilli knew she wasn't totally rational about this subject. It was too close to her heart. She took a shallow
breath and met his gaze. "I don't want you to intimidate
me about this," she said in a quiet voice.

He studied her for a moment, his gaze more curious than threatening. "Okay. Are you open to gentle persuasion?"

"Not if it involves any power plays," she said.

He nodded, stepping closer. "Deal. By the way, I'm hosting a casual business gathering Friday night. It's just a barbecue. Feel free to drop in and fill up a plate."

His closeness made her feel as if he'd set off a dozen mini electrical charges inside her. He lifted his hand to a stray strand of her hair. "Your hair reminds me of your personality."

He looped the strand around one of his fingers and she felt her heart accelerate. "How is that?"

His mouth stretched into a sexy grin. "It's the color of an angel's hair, but the curl shows it's rebellious."

Looking into his eyes, she felt as if she were sinking into a place where she was aware of only him. He was the most dynamic man she'd ever met in her life. She felt totally fascinated and totally out of her league.

Grasping on to that thought, she took a shallow breath and stepped back. It was a move totally motivated by survival. Max De Luca was a powerful force, too powerful for her.

The strand of her hair stretched taut between them. Max hadn't released her. She lifted her hand to unravel her hair from his finger, brushing his skin. "I should go. I don't want to be late," she said and fled out the door, feeling as if she'd been burned.

Max arrived home after going several rounds with Alex Megalos, Director of Domestic Operation and Expansion for Megalos-De Luca Enterprises. Alex had been Max's rival for his current position as Director of Worldwide Operation and Expansion.

Talented and aggressive, Alex was always trying to focus resources and energy in his area. Max, however, was forced to continually remind Alex that he had to consider the big picture.

Alex provided a lot of energy, but he also caused more than his share of heartburn. Suffering from a burning sensation in his gut even now, Max just wanted a quiet peaceful evening and an opportunity to wind down. He headed for the bar downstairs and poured himself a glass of red wine.

Sitting in the darkness of the den, he took a sip and savored the stillness of the moment.

A crashing sound followed by a scream shattered the quiet. Alarm shot through him. Immediately jumping to his feet, he raced upstairs. That had been Lilli's scream. What had happened?

Rounding the corner, he found her on the floor of the nursery surrounded by scattered pieces of a crib and tools.

"What in hell are you doing?"

Dressed in shorts that revealed her long legs, her hair straying from the ponytail in back, she glanced up at him with a scowl. "Trying to put this crib back together. Your moving guys took it apart."

He frowned, entering the room. "They should have put it back together." He reached into his pocket for his cell phone. "I'll get my driver up here immediately. He's excellent, extremely mechanical. He'll put it together in no time."

Scrambling to her feet, she put her hands over his to prevent him from dialing. "No. No."

"Why not?"

"Besides the fact that it's not his job to put together cribs and it's almost ten o'clock," she said, "I want to do it myself."

He stared at her for a long moment. "Why?"

"Because I just do. I put this crib together after I bought it. I should be able to do it now."

"Why is it so important that you be the one to assemble it? The baby isn't going to know."

She lifted her chin. "Someday he will. Someday he will know that his mother loved him so much and was so excited that he was coming that she put her time and energy and money into making a nice place for him."

Her heartfelt determination tugged at something inside him. "That never would have occurred to me. I'm certain my mother didn't assemble my crib. I had a string of nannies and was shipped off to boarding school before my parents divorced."

"My mother could sew and knit and she made blankets and caps and booties for me. I'm going to use some of them on my little one."

"But not anything pink," he said.

She smiled and laughed. "Nothing pink. I have a few white and yellow things. After my father left, it was just my mom and me." She bit her lip. "I wish she was still around. I have a feeling I'm going to have a lot of questions."

"I'm sure you'll do an excellent job and when he goes to boarding school—"

Lilli gaped at him. "I'm not sending my child to boarding school."

"There's no need to automatically reject the idea. A

young man can get an excellent education and important connections at an elite boarding school."

"And they end up with warm, affectionate family ties just like you," she said.

He opened his mouth then closed it. "Mr. Steel haunts me again." He shook his head. "There's no need to discuss boarding school. That's years away."

"Never," she corrected.

He loosened his tie and unfastened the top couple of buttons of his shirt. "Let me help you put this crib together. Where are the instructions?"

Lilli winced. "That's the problem. I threw them away after I put it together the first time."

He couldn't swallow a chuckle at her stymied expression. "Okay, then we'll just look it up on Google."

"Google it?" she echoed. "I never thought of that."

"So I'm good for something," he said in a wry voice. "My laptop is in my quarters. Come on. I still haven't given you that tour. From the way you act toward me, I wonder if you still think I have a woman tied to my bed."

Her face bloomed with color and she groaned. "When are you going to stop teasing me about that?"

"When you stop calling me Mr. Steel," he said and led her to another wing of the house.

When Max opened the door to his suite, all Lilli could do was stare. Lush carpet covered the floor, cushioning every footstep. A gas fireplace featuring a stone mantel provided instant warmth. On either side, stone shelves held books, electronic items and a full bar. A large bed covered with luxury linens provided the centerpiece, but what captured her attention was the dramatic arched window that showed the starry sky in all its glory.

"I have shades to cover them if it's too bright," he said.

"How can you bear to do that? It's so beautiful," she said.

"Thank you. I like it. I also have a flat-screen television that comes down from over that wall." He walked through one door and motioned for her to follow. "Personal gym and lap pool."

Lilli blinked at all the equipment. "But you already have a pool."

"That one is for being lazy. This one is for exercise." He glanced her. "You can use it anytime you like. It's okay to swim during pregnancy, isn't it?"

She nodded. "Yes."

He led her to another room, which held a desk, sofa and more electronic equipment. He turned on his laptop. "There's another office suite downstairs, but I tend to accomplish more up here. Would you like some juice or sparkling water?"

She shook her head. "No. I'm fine. All you need to live in here are a kitchen and washer and dryer."

His lips twitched. "There's a galley kitchen across the hall. Laundry chute in my closet."

Tugging off his tie, he released another shirt button. Lilli was struck by the sight of his tanned fingers against the white shirt. He truly was an amazing male. She wondered how many women had shared his bed. No chains needed for him.

She cleared her throat and tried to move her mind in a different direction as he tapped on the keyboard. "Just curious, but do you even know *how* to do laundry?"

He glanced at her and gave a cryptic smile. "Yes, I know how. We were required to learn in boarding school, along with basic mechanics, financial management, survival skills and cooking."

"You can cook?" she said in disbelief.

"I make a damn good omelet, can broil a steak with the best of them and I was recognized for making the best grilled cheese sandwich in my class."

She couldn't stifle a laugh from his defense of his culinary abilities. "Nothing chocolate in your repertoire?"

He shot her a level glance. "I buy only the best." He looked at the screen. "Here we are. Instructions for assembling your crib."

She joined him to look at the screen, surprised at how fast he'd found the instructions. "How did you know what kind?"

"I looked at the brand and model before I left the nursery." He hit the print button and seconds later, they returned to the nursery armed with instructions.

An hour later, they proclaimed victory as Lilli put in the final screw. "We did it," she said, punchy with excitement. She lifted her hand for a high five. "I hate to say it, but I couldn't have done it without you. Thanks."

"My pleasure," he said, his hair mussed from raking his fingers through it. She'd known he'd spent the entire time itching to do the work himself. He'd offered and insisted every five minutes, but she'd demurred. "If only everything were this easy," he said, offering his hand to help her up from the floor.

Her knees cramped from staying in one position too long, she wobbled as she stood. Strong arms wrapped around her and pulled her against his warm body.

Bracing herself on his arms, she was immediately distracted by the sensation of him, smooth skin over hard muscle. Her breasts pressed against his chest, her belly meshed with his and her thighs just barely touched his trousers.

"Are you okay?" he asked in a low voice.

Her heart pounding a mile a minute, she nodded and barely managed a whisper. "Yes. I guess I sat a little too long."

He slid his hand through her hair, surprising her with the sensual but tender gesture. "You stopped seeing my brother months ago. How is it that you don't have a man in your life now?"

She swallowed hard. "I'm pregnant."

"And no man has approached you?"

"No." She closed her eyes, trying not to sink into a helpless puddle on the floor. He felt so strong, so good. The intimate sound of his low voice both soothed her and wreaked havoc with her nervous system. "I didn't want a man in my life. I don't know if I ever will," she said, remembering how victimized she'd felt.

He gave a low laugh that caught her off guard. "You've got to be kidding."

She looked up at him, searching his face in the low lighting. "No. I'm not."

"Every woman has needs," he said.

"I don't," she told him, because it had seemed all her sexual needs had disappeared. "Not for a long time."

"How can you say that? You're attracted to me," he said and slid his fingertips from her hair to her throat.

"That doesn't mean I want to have sex with you," she said, but her skin was heating and her heart was racing.

"I could make you want to be with me," he said. "I could make you want it more than you ever have."

For a sliver of a moment, she believed him and the possibility sent her into turmoil. She had to shut this down once and for all. She took his hand and put it on her belly. "There will always be this between us," she said. "Always."

Max returned to his suite and poured himself a glass of red wine. There was something electric between him and Lilli. He could feel it in his skin and deeper in his gut. She was a little afraid of him, but still determined to hold her own. That attracted him even more. She was resolved to push him away, but she was fascinated by him. He could see it in the way she looked at him, hear it in her quick intake of breath and he felt it in her response to him.

The passion she tried to hide got to him more than any other woman's overt seduction had. He was still aroused from being so close to her.

Plowing his fingers through his hair, he walked to his office and pulled out another legal proposal from his attorney. After watching what had happened to his brother because his guardian had been permissive and irresponsible, Max couldn't stand the idea of another De Luca plunging down the same path.

He suspected Lilli would never sign a document giving him guardianship unless she became ill, and she might not even sign it under those conditions.

There were other options, though. Other ways to make sure this De Luca was raised properly. His attorney had outlined each of them. Some were more costly than others, and not just in terms of money. Rubbing his chin, he remembered when he'd got the news of his brother's death. The feeling of loss and despair had slammed into him like a concrete wall.

He would never let the same thing happen to another De Luca. Never.

Four

The next evening, after a full day at work, Lilli entered the De Luca house to the sound of jazz music, tinkling glasses and animated conversation. She'd noticed a few extra cars in the driveway, but she hadn't known what to expect once she got inside.

The scent of grilled food permeated the house, making her mouth water and her stomach growl. Then she remembered. This must be the barbecue gathering Max had mentioned the other day. All she wanted was a sandwich and she could fix that herself. Heading for the kitchen, she found two men and two women preparing food and placing it on serving trays.

A large bald man barked orders from one end of the large kitchen island. The man pinned her with his gaze as she approached the island. "No guests in the kitchen, *bella*," he chided and pointed to himself. "Louie can't have you stealing secrets."

This was Max's fabulous chef. She hadn't had a chance to meet him yet because he seemed to cook and disappear.

"I'm not really a guest and I won't steal your secrets. I just want to make a peanut butter sandwich. It won't take a minute."

He gasped in horror. "Peanut butter sandwich, when you can eat this?"

"I need to make this quick," she said, more than ready for the solace and quiet of her room. She stepped behind the island. "I just want to take it to my room. Upstairs."

Louie's eyebrows shot upward. "Upstairs? You are a special friend of Mr. De Luca. Only the best—"

"No, no, I'm sure he doesn't think of me as a special friend."

"I don't know why not," a man said from behind her.

Lilli whipped her head around to look at a tall, muscular man with brown hair and luminescent green eyes. "Alex Megalos," he said with a smile as he stood on the other side of the kitchen island.

"Nice to meet you. Lilli McCall."

His eyes crinkled when he smiled. She liked that. She liked that he smiled at her instead of frowning. But she felt the need to disappear. She didn't want to call attention to herself. "I really should go," she said. "This is a business gathering."

"No reason we can't mix business and pleasure. Let's get you a drink. Come out on the patio."

Lilli shook her head again. "Thank you, but I—"

Max stepped into the kitchen and Lilli felt her heart take an extra beat. "When did the party move in here?"

"Max, you've been holding out on us. How did you lure this angel into your dark castle?"

Max met her gaze and she took a deep breath. A snap of electricity crackled between them. "Just lucky, I guess," he said.

"Well, if you need anyone to take her off your hands," Alex ventured.

Max shot him a sideways glance. "Always competing," he said, then turned to the chef. "Louie, the lady is hungry."

"We can't have that," Louie said and quickly put a plate together.

"Max, don't be so greedy. You've already got Kiki," Alex said. "Share her with the rest of us. She should join us tonight."

Lilli stared at Max in panic.

"If you would like—

"I wouldn't," she said. "Like," she added, gulping and shot Alex an apologetic look. "I'm a little tired. Thanks, though."

"I'm crushed," Alex said. "Maybe I could give you a call when you're rested."

Confusion rolled through her as she watched a beautiful brunette appear from behind him. "Max, sweetheart, you disappeared," the woman said.

He turned to the woman. "Kiki, I'll be back before you finish your next drink. I need to take care of a personal matter."

The woman looked at Lilli and lifted one of her perfectly arched eyebrows. "Is this the personal matter?" She narrowed her eyes.

"I—uh—need to go," Lilli said.

"No need to rush," Alex said.

"Exactly," Kiki said.

Lilli felt as if she were suddenly surrounded by vipers. There were too many competing agendas for her comfort. "All I wanted was a peanut butter sandwich," she murmured.

Kiki snickered. "How charming."

"Here's your plate, bella," Louie said.

"Bless you," she said. "Thank you. It looks delicious." She turned to Alex and Kiki. "It was nice to meet you. Have a lovely evening."

"I will," Kiki said and slid her hand around Max's well-developed bicep.

Lilli nodded, feeling an odd combination of emotions, most of which she didn't want to examine. "Good night," she said and stepped from behind the kitchen island.

Kiki's jaw dropped. Alex blinked.

They were looking at her pregnant belly.

"Want Lilli all to yourself for the rest of the evening?" Max asked, shooting Alex a sly grin. He winked at Lilli and his humor helped her get through the incredibly awkward moment.

"Uh…uh…" Alex seemed unable to pry his gaze from her belly. He cleared his throat and closed his eyes then forced his gaze upward. He exhaled and smiled. "Hell, I bet she would be more fun than you are. And trust me, Lilli, I'm a lot more fun than Max."

"Who is the lucky father?" Kiki asked in a strained voice.

Lilli glanced at Max. "Um, it's—"

He met her gaze. "That's between me and Lilli."

Kiki's face tightened with suspicion. "That's a little vague, darling," she said with an edge to her tone.

"Kiki, this is not the place for this discussion," he said. "Louie will be upset if we don't enjoy his meal. I'll talk to you later," he said, looking at Lilli.

"That's okay," she said, feeling her nerves jump in her stomach. "I'm hitting the sack early tonight. Very tired. Thank you again, Louie. G'night. Enjoy your evening," she said and scooted out of the room, thankful that Kiki wasn't armed. Otherwise, she was certain she would be so dead.

While Lilli ate, she watched a boring show on her flat-screen television. Afterward, she took a shower and went to bed, but didn't fall asleep. Pulling a book about newborn care from her nightstand, she added to the list of items she would need to purchase for the baby.

A knock sounded on her door and she tensed, but didn't answer. The knock sounded again and she held her breath.

"I know you're not asleep," Max said. "I heard you walking around three minutes ago."

Lilli frowned. She'd gotten a drink of water from the attached bathroom. Sighing, she rose from the bed and opened the door.

Max stepped inside and closed the door behind him. His gaze fell over her body, and he gave her a bottle of water and a cookie. "You've charmed my chef. Louie said you looked like you could use a cookie."

"Thank you," she said, appreciating his kindness. "But I'm sure it's because he thinks I'm a special friend of yours, even though I told him I'm not."

"It's safe to say we have a special relationship," he said. "A bond, in a way."

His tone made her stomach dip. "Speaking of special friends," she said. "Just curious, was there a particular reason you didn't tell Kiki the real father of my child?"

"Yes. For safety reasons, I've decided it's better not to comment on your relationship with Tony. There are too many people he owes."

"Oh," she said, remembering the threat and feeling a sinking sensation in her stomach. She sat down on the bed. "I keep trying to forget about that."

"Don't," he said, moving toward her. "You need to be on guard when you go out in public. People will try to take advantage of you if they know of your association with the De Lucas."

"I don't think my real friends would dream of taking advantage of me," she said and put the cookie and bottle of water on the nightstand. The soft glow of the bedside lamp intensified the intimacy of the moment. He was close enough that she could smell a hint of his cologne and masculine scent. She could almost feel him.

He gave a cynical smile. "People will always try to take advantage of you when you have money."

"You forget," she said. "I don't really have any money."

He sat down beside her on the bed and studied her. "That could change," he said.

Feeling his gaze on her, she looked at him. The expression on his face affected her in a strange way. "How?"

"There are options," he said.

"If this involves that crazy contract," she began.

"We won't discuss it at this late hour," he said. "Alex

asked me to give you his card. He couldn't stop talking about you."

"That didn't have anything to do with me," she said, her hair drooping over one of her eyes. "I could tell he was only interested because he liked the idea of taking something away that he thought was yours. Just a game."

"You're right that Alex is very competitive with me, but you underestimate your appeal," he said and lifted his hand to her hair.

Her heart fluttered. She could have pushed him away if she'd had the inclination, but she couldn't find it anywhere inside her. He slid his hand over her cheek and then down to her mouth, rubbing his thumb over her bottom lip.

Her skin tingled everywhere he touched. She swallowed hard. "Why are you touching me?"

"You don't like it?" he asked, his dark gaze meeting hers. "There are so many reasons you should be off-limits." He moved closer. "But I like the way your skin feels. I like the way you look at me when I touch you."

She inhaled a shallow breath and caught another draft of his spicy scent mixed with cologne. In some corner of her mind, it occurred to her that she'd never been this close to such a powerful man. He knew who he was and what he had to do, and he was the kind of man who would make whatever he wanted a reality.

For Lilli, it was like getting up close and personal with a wild tiger. At the same time, he was solid and strong and she knew he would never force a woman. He wouldn't need to. And to have him looking at her as his object of desire made her dizzy.

"There's something about you," he said, gently urging her mouth open so he could slide his thumb just inside to her tongue. "Wide blue eyes with secrets, a sweet smile." He glanced downward. "You make me curious."

Lilli was shocked at how quickly her body responded. She'd considered herself sexually dead, but she felt her skin heat and the tips of her breasts tighten against her white cotton gown.

He saw it, too. She knew it by the expression on his face.

"I shouldn't want you," he muttered and slid his hand around the back of her neck. "But dammit, I do." He lowered his mouth to hers and took her lips in a kiss that made her lose track of time and space.

His tongue slid over hers and she felt herself respond. It was all instinctual. Her heart pounded in her head and her blood pooled in secret, sensitive places. Every second that she felt his warmth, his touch, she was shocked by her immediate response to him. Something inside her could not push him away.

She felt him lower one of his hands to her breast. Air caught somewhere in her throat as he caressed her through her gown. He rubbed the palm of his hand over the side of her breast and she shivered, pressing up against him.

He gave a low groan of approval and drew his hand closer to her nipple, but not quite touching it. She felt the peak of it stiffen against her nightgown, aching for his touch.

Full of wanting, she held her breath.

He finally pushed the top of her gown down and slid his thumb over her nipple. She couldn't swallow a moan of relief with a twinge of frustration.

He pulled his mouth from hers and slid his lips over her skin, down her throat and collarbone. A riot of sensations shot through her. She wanted him everywhere at once.

His other hand slid over her back, massaging her, holding her in a solid embrace. The combination of security and caresses hit her physically and emotionally.

He looked up at her, dark desire in his eyes. Swearing under his breath, he shook his head.

Pulling back, he rose from the bed and prowled toward the window. Moonlight spilled over his profile as he raked his hand through his hair.

Lilli drank in a gulp of air, trying to clear her head. Shocked at herself, she tugged her gown back in place and tried to make sense of what had just happened. That night after she'd broken up with Tony, the night made doubly awful because she couldn't recall it, she'd changed. She'd known she would never be the same. She would never be able to let a man touch her again unless she trusted him.

Why should she trust Max? There was no good reason. But something inside her did. Either that or she was crazier than she'd thought she was.

"You're so responsive. I wonder…were you this responsive with my brother," he ventured in a low voice.

"I wasn't," she said, the words popping out before she could stop them.

He turned to look at her. "Why not?"

She bit her lip. "I can't explain it. It's just different."

He continued to hold her gaze. "Did you leave my brother before or after you found out you were pregnant?"

"Before." She looked away from him. "Something happened one night. I knew I couldn't stay."

"What was it?"

"I don't like talking about it," she said, twisting her fingers together. "I knew I had to get away from him and his—" her stomach clenched with nausea "—his world."

"And you weren't tempted to go back with him when you found out you were pregnant?"

She shook her head vehemently. "Oh, absolutely not. If I didn't belong in his world, there was no way a baby would."

"Did he ask you back?"

She nodded. "Several times. But I think he was relieved when I said no. Tony wasn't ready to be a father."

"What about the baby? What will you do about a father figure for him?"

"I'll deal with that later. Right now, I need to get through the pregnancy and delivery. My girlfriends have promised to help me through the scary first few months." She felt a sense of dread in the pit of her stomach. "Then I guess I'll have to move."

Feeling his gaze on her, she looked up at him, wondering what he was thinking, what judgments he was making. "You probably don't understand any of this. How I could end up with your brother and then pregnant with no husband? You would never get yourself into such a crazy situation because you don't let emotions make your decisions."

"You're completely correct."

"I'm also completely human. Are you?"

His mouth lifted in a half smile. "Unfortunately, yes. Human enough to want to finish what we started a few minutes ago." He moved toward her, and she felt her heart jump into her throat. "Don't worry. I won't. I may be human, but I'm not ruled by my hormones. Good night, Lilli."

Staring after him in surprise, she took a ragged breath. She felt totally off balance.

I'm human, but I'm not ruled by my hormones.

That was part of the reason she'd responded to him. She had a gut feeling that he had maintained control of himself. He wouldn't lose it unless he chose to do so. She'd never been around such a man but she could sense it about him and it made her feel secure at the same time that it knocked her sideways. She closed her eyes and pushed her hair from her face. She needed to stay on guard.

Five

Lilli's hands were shaking as she turned onto Max's street Saturday after working at the free dental clinic. She'd been so careful at work lately, always making sure to have someone walk her to her car. Afterward, she'd stopped to visit Devon Jones, one of the hospice workers who had helped her mother during her last days. Devon was now caring for his own father during the end stages of a long illness.

After she'd left, she'd noticed a black car in her rearview mirror. Even after making a few turns, the car remained behind her. She became so nervous that she'd taken some wrong turns and had got lost.

Glancing over her shoulder as she pulled into the driveway, she shook her head. Surely they wouldn't follow her all the way to Max's house. Biting her lip, she grabbed her purse and rushed into the house, leaning against the door as she closed it, and took a deep breath. She closed her eyes for a moment to calm herself. When she opened them, Max was five feet away from her, pinning her with a searching gaze.

"And you look like you've had some excitement," he said. "Anything you want to tell me?"

She tried to shrug, but shivered instead. Despite the way he'd left her feeling last night, she couldn't deny feeling ten times safer in his presence. "Not right now," she said and headed for the kitchen. "Water sounds good."

Her heart still racing, she took another deep breath and put her hand to her chest.

"Lilli," he said from behind her and she thought she heard a note of concern in his voice. Hallucinating, she told herself. "Are you okay?"

"I will be," she insisted, getting a glass and filling it with filtered water from the refrigerator.

He moved in front of her and studied her. "Where have you been?"

"Work, well, not really work," she corrected.

"Your office isn't open on Saturday," he said, his expression growing suspicious.

"That's right. But we volunteer for the free clinic downtown. I filled in for one of the other hygienists."

"Downtown? Where?" he asked, clearly not pleased.

She winced. She had expected he wouldn't approve of her driving downtown by herself, but no one had bothered her for days.

She told him the address and his mouth tightened. "Afterward, I stopped by to check on a hospice assistant who worked with my mother." She shook her head. "Poor Devon. His own father is dying now."

"Devon? What did this guy want? Did he ask you for anything?"

"No, but if he did, I would try to help him. He helped my mother and I during a very difficult time."

"This is what I warned you about. You need to be careful because people will come out of the woodwork playing on your sympathy and asking for *help*."

"That hasn't happened," she said, folding her arms over her chest.

"Then what happened to make you so upset? Did one of Tony's buddies show up?"

"Aside from getting lost, the only thing I can tell you is that someone in a black Mercedes followed me most of the way home."

He swore under his breath. "That's it. You're quitting."

She gaped at him. "Quitting?"

"It's the only rational thing to do. Each day that passes I learn more about how deeply Tony was in trouble. You can stay here until the baby is born and you're ready to move and say goodbye to your contacts here. I've told you before. You need to be on guard in every way. People will try to take advantage of you."

She shook her head. "I can't quit. I need the income for the baby. As you said, babies aren't cheap."

"Money won't be a concern after you sign the agreement."

She supposed she should have been intimidated by him and part of her was, but she refused to give in to it. "I'm not signing that stupid agreement and I'm not taking your money."

"You would turn down a good life for your child in exchange for pride."

She scowled at him. "That was low. The point is that I'm not giving control of my child to you or anyone else. I don't know you well enough. You may give the impression of being very responsible, but at the same time you're bitter, cynical and a workaholic. I want my butter bean to be happy. You may be loaded, but you don't seem very happy."

"Butter bean?" he repeated.

"Yes, butter bean. An affectionate nickname. Something you wouldn't understand."

Exasperation crossed his handsome face. "Most women would kill to have the equivalent of an extended vacation here, but you're fighting it every inch of the way. Have you always been this disagreeable?"

"I think you just bring it out in me," she said.

"Do you have a will?"

"Yes, I do," she said.

"Have you chosen a guardian for you child?"

She resisted the urge to squirm. "I'm working on it."

"Why don't you name me the guardian?" he demanded.

She bit her lip. "Because you don't smile enough." As soon as she blurted out her answer, she knew it sounded a little crazy. "I think kids need smiles and lots of hugs."

He moved toward her. "I think you trust me more than you admit."

Her heart flipped. Maybe she did. There was something so solid about him. "I trust you to be rational, but some decisions should be more emotional."

He lifted an eyebrow. "Are you saying your emotional decisions have turned out well?"

"Not all, obviously," she said. "But it was at least partly an emotional decision for me to take a leave of absence from work to take care of my mother during her last months. I wouldn't trade anything for the time I had with her, because I won't have a chance for that again."

A trace of sympathy softened his hard gaze.

"If you were my son's guardian, what would you do if you had to choose between attending an important business meeting or going to his T-ball game?" She shrugged. "I'm going to make a wild guess and say you'd choose the former because it would be the more rational decision."

"You make a good point, but most parents have to balance career and children's needs. There's no reason I couldn't learn to do the same thing."

She crossed her arms over her chest. "How would you do that?"

He looked surprised that she would question him. "Why do I feel as if I'm being interviewed for a position?"

She nodded. "Maybe you are," she said. "You've pretty much asked, no, demanded to be the baby's guardian in case of my death or path to self-destruction. If someone asked you to give them the most important job in the world, wouldn't you interview them? Probably conduct a background search. Ask for references."

He gave an incredulous laugh, his teeth gleaming brightly in contrast to his tanned skin. "I don't know whether to be offended or—" A cell phone rang and his smile fell. He pulled the phone from his pocket and checked the number. "Excuse me," he murmured. "Yes, Rena?" He paused and shook his head. "I've sent a donation for the event tonight, but won't be attending." He listened for a moment. "I'm sorry they'll be disappointed. Hopefully the money I sent will soothe some of their pain. Okay. Have a good day."

He turned off the phone and turned back to Lilli. "Sorry that was my cousin Rena. She thinks I'm a recluse and she's determined to get me more socially involved."

"But you don't want to," Lilli included.

"This will be a boring chicken dinner with a silent auction afterward. I get enough social involvement at work. And I'm not stingy with my donations."

"But maybe Rena thinks that more people would be more generous with their contributions if they actually saw you show up at the charitable functions sometimes. You would be a good example," she said.

"Maybe," he said, clearly not convinced. "Do you know how painful these things can be?"

"Probably not," she said. "But it's not like you're making a lifetime commitment."

He sighed and met her gaze. "Okay, I'll tell you what. I'll go to the fund-raiser for the children's wing of the hospital if you'll go with me."

"Me?" she said, shocked. "But I'm pregnant."

"Does that mean you're disabled?"

"No, but—" she shook her head "—why would you want me to go? You're bound to have a dozen other women on the line who would want to go with you."

"Meaning you wouldn't," he said in a dry, amused tone.

"I didn't say that," he said. "What about Kiki?"

"I didn't invite Kiki," he said. "I invited you."

Her heart sped up. She cleared her throat. "I don't have anything to wear."

"I can have someone take care of that within an hour."

He was shredding her protests more effectively than a paper shredder. She stared at him, her mind spinning.

"Think of it as an opportunity to continue your interview," he said, as if he weren't at all worried that he would meet and exceed her expectations.

Must be nice to have that kind of confidence, she thought. "This is crazy. I can't believe you want to take me to this kind of event. Aren't you concerned about the gossip?"

"With my father, his mistress and my brother, I've been dealing with gossip most of my life. This will be a cakewalk."

Lilli took a shower and as she was fixing her hair, a knock sounded on her door. She opened it to Max's housekeeper, Myrtle, who held a large box. "For you," the older woman with iron-gray hair said and carried the box to the bed.

"Already?" Lilli asked, glancing at the clock. When Max said an hour, he meant an hour. "Thank you very much, Myrtle," she said, opening the box and pushing aside layers of tissue paper. "Omigoodness, this is beautiful. Did you see it?" she asked the chief housekeeper. She held up the black gown with the fitted bodice and deep V-neck. Just under the bustline dotted with tiny embroidered pink flowers, the remainder of the dress fell in a swirl of silk.

The woman nodded. "It's beautiful. Perfect for you. Mr. De Luca is always very generous."

"Yes, he is, isn't he?" She looked in vain for a price tag, wishing she could reimburse him for the dress. "Do you think he would let me pay him—"

Before she even finished, Myrtle shook her head. "Never," she said.

Sighing, she met Myrtle's gaze. "I don't want to be on the long list of people who sponge off of him."

Myrtle gave a slight smile that softened her usual stern expression. "You will have a difficult time outgiving Mr. De Luca."

Lilli frowned thoughtfully. "How long have you worked for Mr. De Luca?"

"Six years. One of those years, my husband was ill and he allowed me extra time off with pay. I'll always be grateful to him for that."

"I don't know how to ask this, but does Mr. De Luca have any *real* friends?"

"Very few," Myrtle said. "He keeps very busy with his company and socializes very little. And there are his godchildren."

Lilli blinked. "Godchildren? I didn't know he was a godfather."

"With such wealth, he's a natural choice. I should go," she said. "You'll look beautiful in your dress. Mr. De Luca would want you to enjoy it."

"Just on more thing," Lilli said as the woman headed for the door. "When is Mr. De Luca's birthday?"

"Next month, the fifth," she said. "But he never celebrates it."

Lilli's mind immediately flew with possibilities. *He*

never celebrates it. Well, maybe this year should be different. And he was a godfather? Who would have guessed? Sheesh, she should talk to Myrtle more often.

She glanced at the clock again and felt a kick of nerves. She would think about that later. Now she needed to get ready for the charity dinner. She wanted the rest of her to measure up to that beautiful dress.

It occurred to Lilli that perhaps she could have used a team of hairstylists and consultants to get her up to snuff for this event. Instead she would need to rely on the cosmetic tips she'd gleaned from the last fashion magazine she'd read and that had been two or three months ago.

One hour and ten minutes later, Max checked his watch again and wondered if he should sit down and review some reports while he waited for Lilli. Just as he headed for his downstairs office, she appeared at the top of the stairs. He stared for a long moment as she descended the steps. Her blond hair flowing in loose spiral curls to her shoulders and fair skin made her look like an angel. The cut of her black halter dress dipped into a deep V that drew his gaze to her breasts, and the way the fabric bonded lovingly to her curves made him hard.

Her pregnancy was obvious. The dress made no attempt to hide it. He wondered why he was so attracted to this woman. It made no sense at all, especially knowing the baby she carried belonged to his dead brother.

He clenched his teeth and nodded. "You look lovely."

"Thank you," she said with a smile. "So do you."

His lips twitched. He chuckled. "Thanks." He extended his elbow. "Ready?"

"As ever," she murmured and slid her arm through his. "You can still back out if you want. I mean, unless you've changed your mind about having me tag along."

"Not a chance," he said, guiding her through the doorway. "You're not backing out, are you?"

She shot him a sideways glance. "Not a chance. It's not as if I'm ever going to see these people again."

"You never know," he said, escorting her to the luxury sedan parked out front. He opened the car door for her. "You may enjoy yourself."

"I just hope the food is good. If it's not, we can always stop for a cheeseburger with everything on the way home."

He just grinned and got into the car. Adjusting the sound system to play an operatic aria, he noticed Lilli began to fidget after a few minutes. "Problem?" he asked.

"No, no, not really," she said, pushing her hair behind her shoulder as she moved her foot in a staccato beat at odds with the aria. He heard the soft jangle of her anklet with every movement. It was difficult to keep his gaze from straying to her sexy legs.

"Are you sure there's nothing wrong?" he asked.

"Do you know what she's saying?" she asked, pointing toward the CD player.

"It's from a German opera by Mozart called *The Magic Flute*. I didn't study much German, but if I remember correctly, she's saying something along the lines of 'The vengeance of hell boils in my heart. Death and despair flame about me.'"

"Cheerful little ditty, huh," she said. "That's why I'm not crazy about opera. Someone is usually pissed off, plotting to kill someone or getting killed."

"True. But some are more upbeat than others. I'll

have to take you sometime," he said, amused at the image of sharing such an experience with Lilli. "Have you thought about what kind of music is good for the baby's development?"

She nodded vigorously. "I want him to enjoy a variety of music, so I play instrumental Mozart for him. Based on what you just told me about the translation to that aria, I think I'll skip most opera for a while. I've also already started him on the Baby Einstein series."

"You've done some research," he said and felt the weight of her gaze on him.

"You sound surprised."

"Maybe I was," he admitted. "Since this pregnancy was unplanned—"

"Doesn't mean I'm not going to be informed. I've signed up to take an infant care class in a couple of weeks, and I've been researching pediatricians. Since I've changed where I'm living, I may need to do some additional research."

"I can get you the best pediatrician in Las Vegas any-time you want," he said finally, determined that Lilli and his nephew would have no less. "What kind of preschool you want him to attend?"

"I'm leaning toward a Montessori school but they can be expensive, so I'll have to see."

"Money won't be an issue—"

"As long as I sign your agreement, which I won't," she said.

"Yet," he corrected, feeling a twist of impatience. He'd made sure he didn't do anything that would cause his character to be called into question. Not after his father. "You can change your mind after you know me better."

"Maybe," she conceded. "But I still don't like the idea of signing my butter bean over to anyone."

"It's the job of a parent to make sure the child is taken care of in the event of the parent's death."

"I know."

A swollen silence followed, and he sensed she was thinking about things that made her sad. His gut twisted. He couldn't explain it, but he didn't want Lilli sad, so he changed the subject. "You didn't say anything about sports. The De Lucas are naturally athletic, good with any competitive sports. I could teach him soccer, tennis, basketball."

"That's nice, but the important question is can you play peekaboo?"

Max blinked and glanced at her. From the glow of the dashboard, her eyes gleamed with a combination of innocence and sensuality. "Peekaboo?"

She nodded. "Yes, and how good are you at giving hugs and pats on the back? A kid needs hugs and pats on the back more than soccer."

Max digested her comments for a long moment. "You think I may not be affectionate enough."

"I didn't actually say that."

"But you thought it."

She opened her mouth then closed it. "I think a child needs someone who means safety and security, home. That person will love you whether you make the goal or not. That person will teach you how to take a bad day and make it better. I think a child needs compassion."

He pulled in front of the resort where the event was being hosted. "We'll continue this discussion later."

"Okay," she said and lifted her mouth in a sexy smile. "Are you ready for your grand entrance?"

He looked at her for a long moment, unable to tear his gaze away from her. With her sunbeam hair and eyes full of life, she literally sparkled. She took his breath away. "Sweetheart, they're not going to be looking at me," he said, and gave his keys to the valet.

Six

Lilli felt curious gazes fastened on her as she sat next to Max at the dinner table. Chandeliers lit the luxurious ballroom, warming the red carpet and creating a glow on faces belonging to the who's who of the Las Vegas elite. Walls lined with elegant mirrors reflected women outfitted in designer gowns swishing alongside men dressed in expertly tailored suits. Servers refilled her glass of water before she had an opportunity to make a request.

It was by far the most luxurious event she'd ever attended and she constantly reminded herself not to put her elbows on the table. She noticed many people made a point of stopping to speak to Max. Even the mistress of ceremonies introduced him and thanked him for donating the resort's grand ballroom for the night's festivities.

Just as Max picked up his fork to take a bite of coq

au vin, a man stopped and touched his shoulder. "Good to see you here, Max. And congrats on the success of your latest refurbishment project in your Luxotic resorts in the Caribbean. I understand they're often booked over a year in advance."

"Thank you," Max said. "It takes a team. Good to see you too, Robert."

The man walked away and Lilli leaned toward Max and whispered, "Would you like me to put a sign on the back of your chair telling people not to talk to you until you finish eating?"

His lips twitched. "There are only three words appropriate for that question."

"What?"

"I told you," he said and took a bite.

"True," she said. "But maybe people wouldn't feel it necessary to try to talk to you if you attended more of these. Think about it. If they know this is their only shot at actually speaking to the mighty Max De Luca, they've got to grab it. If, however, they know you'll show up at some other events, maybe they won't feel the need to speak to you every time they see you, which is almost never."

"You're saying the attraction to me is how rarely I appear. It has nothing to do with me or my position. If I showed up more often, I would be old news."

She realized he could take that as an insult. "I never used the word *old news*. I'm just saying maybe some of the attention could be spread out over several appearances instead of concentrated on just one."

"Spread the torture out over several evenings instead of getting it done in one."

She sighed and shook her head. "Maybe it wouldn't feel as much like torture if it was spread out." She glanced up and saw a familiar woman walking toward them. "Is that—"

"Max, what a surprise. You told me you weren't planning to come tonight," the woman said and Lilli recalled who she was. Kiki.

Lilli felt a nervous twitch at the back of her neck.

"Last-minute change of plans," Max said, rising to his feet. "Are you enjoying the event?"

Kiki shot Lilli a venomous glance. "Not as much as if I were with you," she said and touched his arm.

"Oh, I'm sure I would have bored you to tears. I'm doing the same to Lilli. Just ask her," he said, glancing down at Lilli with a devil's glint in his eyes.

"I'm sure *Lilli* would never call you boring," Kiki said. "No woman in her right mind would."

"Let's ask Lilli. Tell the truth," he said.

She searched his gaze, wondering why on earth he was putting her on the spot like this. "Kiki is right. I wouldn't have described you as boring."

"See?" Kiki said.

"But he can complain right up there with the best of them," she added.

Kiki's eyes narrowed in disapproval. Max stared at her in surprise and Lilli heard the clatter of sterling silver hit the floor beside her followed by the sound of nervous laughter from the woman sitting in the chair beside her.

Fighting a twinge of nervousness and regret, Lilli lifted her shoulders. "You told me to be honest."

"Yes, I did," he said, giving the distinct impression he wouldn't make the same request again.

Kiki cleared her throat. "I need a quick private word with you, Max. It's urgent. Do you mind?"

He shot a longing glance at his food and Lilli. "Oh, go," she urged him. "If you're not back soon, I'll ask the server to wrap it up to take home."

He bent down and whispered in her ear. "At this rate we may be stopping at Wendy's for me."

She smiled. "Drive-through is open until midnight."

He gave a rough chuckle and turned toward Kiki.

"He's so hot," the young woman beside her said. "How could you send him off with that beautiful woman? You must be confident of your relationship with him," she said in admiration.

Lilli turned to the pudgy young woman with the sweet face. "Max and I have an unusual relationship," she said wryly.

The woman nodded, glancing at Lilli's pregnant belly. "You don't have to tell me anything. I've heard him dodging questions the entire dinner. I know what it's like to be surrounded by people with hidden agendas. Oh, I'm sorry. I should have introduced myself. I'm Mallory James."

"I'm Lilli—"

"McCall," Mallory said, then blushed. "I overheard him introduce you several times. I'm not usually nosy, but since I'm here by myself tonight, and the two of you were more interesting than the almost-dead and completely deaf eighty-seven-year-old beside me…well…"

Lilli smiled. "I'm glad we at least provided a little entertainment. Nice to meet you, Mallory."

The other woman glanced past Lilli's shoulder. "Good grief, you're surrounded by them," she murmured.

"Lilli, you're looking delicious tonight," a male voice said just behind her.

Lilli turned around to meet Alex Megalos's friendly gaze. She couldn't help smiling as she shook her head. "Do you give lessons on flirting on the side?"

"No way. Gotta keep my edge. Where did Max go? Not wise to abandon a woman as beautiful as you."

"You're so right," she said. "I'm bracing myself for the stampede any minute."

Mallory cleared her throat loudly.

Lilli glanced back at the woman whose expression clearly said *please introduce me.* "Oh, Alex Megalos, have you met Mallory James? She's new to town. Alex works for Megalos-De Luca Enterprises."

Alex extended his hand to Mallory and lifted it to his lips. "Enchanted. Have I heard of your father?"

"Perhaps," Mallory said, stuttering. "James Investments and Wealth Management."

Alex nodded in recognition and gave a roguish smile, dipping his head toward hers. "Yes. I bet he keeps you under lock and key. I hear he's excellent. I'd love a chance to chat with him. Is he here tonight?"

"Not tonight," Mallory said and pulled out a card. "But I'd be happy to introduce you. Give me a call?" she asked, rising, bumping into a server carrying a tray of drinks.

"Oh, no." Lilli watched helplessly as the drinks tumbled, splattering Mallory's pink gown and at least one leg of Alex's pants.

The server's face froze. "I'm so sorry."

"Club soda," Lilli said, quickly standing. "Club soda works magic for stains. And we need more napkins," she called after the waiter as he left. She gave her napkin to Alex and blindly accepted one that someone else offered her.

She gave the other napkin to Mallory, meeting the horrified gaze of her new acquaintance. "Mallory, go ahead to the powder room. I'll bring the club soda, sweetheart. These servers move so quickly," she said.

As soon as Mallory was out of earshot, she turned to Alex. "Shame on you for causing all this trouble."

"Me?" Alex said in an incredulous voice, wiping his slacks.

"You're such a flirt. I'm sure you know what kind of effect you have on most women. You really should be more careful doling out those kisses and smiles."

Max appeared at her side and glanced at Alex. "Did someone finally decide to douse him?" he asked, half-joking.

Alex met Max's gaze and gave a heavy sigh. "No. it was the server. Dammit, Lilli can explain it to you," he said and left.

"He didn't hit on you again, did he?"

She shook her head. "He's a flirt. I introduced him to the woman beside me and he got her all flustered. She bumped into the server and there was a spill. Ah, here comes the club soda," she said, smiling at the server as he delivered the bottle and some extra napkins.

"I'm so sorry," he said.

"Accidents happen," she said then looked at Max. "I need to do a little emergency stain removal."

"Saving the day?" he said, his gaze glinting with something that looked like approval.

"That's a stretch, but I would hope someone would do the same for me in the same situation."

He lowered his head toward her. "I could kiss you right this very minute."

Lilli's heart slammed into her rib cage and she gaped at Max. "You—"

"You heard me," he said and his voice was so seductive she immediately felt hot and flustered. "Now go do your good deed."

Stepping backward, her gaze still trapped by his, she nearly stumbled. Max's hand shot out to steady her. "You're worse than Alex."

His eyes widened in outrage. "What the hell—"

She pulled away. "I need to do my good deed," she said and forced her gaze away from his so she could regain her equilibrium. *Men,* she thought and headed for the powder room.

As soon as she entered the luxurious room with a sitting area separate from the stalls, she looked for Mallory, but couldn't find her. Lilli walked into the connecting room filled with stalls and tentatively called, "Mallory?"

"I'm here," she said, covering her face as she exited one of the restrooms. "I can't believe I did that. I'm so embarrassed. I can't go back in there."

"Of course you can. It was just a little spill. They happen all the time," Lilli said, urging the young woman into the sitting area. "Come on. Let me work on your dress."

Mallory moaned. "Why did I have to make a server spill wine on the most amazing man I've ever met?"

"Alex can afford to be taken down a peg or two." She poured a little club soda on the worst spots.

"But not by me," Mallory said. "Do you think he'll run from me every time he sees me from now on?"

Lilli shook her head, dabbing at the dress. "Of course he won't. If nothing else, your meeting was memorable. He'll probably talk to dozens of people tonight, but not many—"

"None," Mallory corrected and gave a reluctant laugh. "None will have gotten his slacks wet." She smiled and met Lillie's gaze. "You've been very kind to me. Would you mind getting together with me sometime for lunch if I promise to try not to spill anything on you?"

Lilli laughed. "I'd love to," she said. "You know this is the same kind of thing that could have happened to me."

"I can't see it," Mallory said. "You look so graceful."

"Thank you, but it's true. Now it's time for us to get back to dinner. The auction should start soon."

Mallory sighed and stood. "Okay, let me put on a little more lipstick."

While Mallory took a couple extra minutes to primp, Lilli walked out into the hallway. She'd gone no more than three steps when she nearly ran into Kiki.

Lilli immediately backed away. "Oh, excuse me. How are you?"

Kiki narrowed her eyes. "I could be a lot better." She stared at Lilli for a long moment then cocked her head to the other less busy side of the hallway. "Do you have a moment? I'd like to talk with you."

"I probably should get back to—"

"Max," Kiki said, her beautiful face tightening with displeasure. "He can wait. This won't take long."

Lilli reluctantly followed Kiki.

"You probably don't know this, but Max and I have

a very close relationship. *Very* close," she emphasized. "In fact, no one would be surprised if we were to get married. We've been seeing each other for a couple of years."

Lilli nodded. "I see."

"A man like Max, well, a woman just has to accept that he may stray every now and then. It doesn't really mean anything. Men, especially powerful men, have women throwing themselves at them all the time."

Lilli wondered what this had to do with her.

"Now Max hasn't wanted to admit anything," Kiki continued with a determined smile that didn't reach her eyes. "I'm sure he doesn't want to hurt my feelings. But I'm not stupid. He obviously feels obligated toward you and I can understand why you would want to take advantage of the situation."

"Not really," Lilli said.

Kiki waved her hand. "You don't need to deny it. I can't imagine any woman in your position who wouldn't exploit the situation to her advantage."

Lilli felt a spurt of anger. "I'm—"

"Just hear me out," Kiki interjected. "What you need to understand is that you won't be able to hold him. Sure, he'll be a great father to the child, but Max is a special man and trust me, he requires special handling. I know he will provide financial support for your child. But you seem like an independent-minded woman, so I thought you might like some additional support of your own."

Confusion and wariness mixed inside her. "Additional support?"

Kiki lowered her voice. "Here's the deal. You leave

Max, never come back and don't get in my way and I'll give you fifty thousand dollars."

Lilli blinked at the woman in disbelief. "Are you serious?"

"Dead serious," Kiki said. "Max is very important to me."

Incredulous, Lilli shook her head. "I can't—"

"Sure you can. Think about it. Imagine getting all that money and a clean break to do what you want where you want." She paused a half beat. "If you make the move within a week, I might even throw in a bonus. You could buy yourself a little condo or house and be in charge of your own life. Trust me, if you stay with Max, he'll have an opinion about everything you say and do." She pressed a card into Lilli's hand. "Call me. I'll make it worth your while."

Lilli stared after the woman as she strode away. She couldn't believe what had just happened. The conversation ran through her mind again, but it was almost too much for her to comprehend.

"Hey, Lilli," Mallory said, moving her hand in front of Lilli's face. "Are you okay? You look a little sick. Should you sit down?"

Lilli shook her head to clear it. "No, I just—" She sighed and headed back to the table.

"Are you sure?" Mallory asked as she followed after her. "You look pale. Like you're sick or you just had a close encounter with an alien or something. Some people don't believe in that stuff, but I do."

Lilli shook her head at the irony. "That's a pretty good explanation," she said.

"What is?" Mallory asked.

"A close encounter with an alien," Lilli said, crumpling Kiki's card into a little wad and tossing it onto a passing waiter's empty tray.

Mallory nodded and whispered, "The place is full of aliens tonight, isn't it?"

Still shaken from her encounter with Kiki, but trying to get past it, Lilli returned with Mallory to the table just as dessert was being served. Max immediately stood and helped both Lilli and Mallory into their chairs while Lilli introduced Mallory.

After they all sat down, he turned to Lilli. "Everything okay?"

She gave a circular nod, but mustered a smile.

"You want to explain that remark about Alex?" he asked.

She felt her cheeks heat with embarrassment. "I was just commenting that it's not fair for him—or you—to use your—" she searched for an appropriate word "—appeal to put a woman off balance."

His lips twitched. "Are you admitting I put you off balance?"

She reached for her glass of water. "I'm not saying anything else. I offered my explanation."

"Sounds like you're pleading the fifth."

"How is Kiki?" she asked, changing the focus off herself.

Irritation crossed his face. "How is it that a woman can appear perfectly sane and rational at the beginning of a relationship then turn totally insane and irrational at the end?"

"It's all the man's fault," she said. "Men turn women

into raging lunatics. They hint, they promise, they mislead."

"I am always up-front in my relationships with women. I make it clear that I'm not interested in marriage and—"

"Why not?" she asked. "Why aren't you interested in marriage?"

"It needs to be the right woman at the right time. I've never found the right woman."

"Why not Kiki?" she asked, keeping her voice low.

"This isn't the best place for a private discussion, but I've never been serious about Kiki. She's a beautiful, intelligent woman, but not right for me in the long run. I told her that from the beginning."

Ouch, Lilli thought. That couldn't have gone over well. "Is there anything you did that might have led her to believe that you'd changed your mind and that you and her were getting close to a commitment?"

He narrowed his eyes. "Why are you asking these questions?"

She shrugged. "Just curious. She seems a little…"

"A little what?"

"I don't know. Maybe possessive."

"I made it clear tonight that we're through. Now, don't you want to eat some of this dessert? It's chocolate cake."

Lilli's stomach twisted. "I'd love to, but I'm full."

He studied her for a long moment. "Something's not right," he began.

"Ladies and gentleman," Ann Wingate, the mistress of ceremonies announced, saving Lilli from replying to Max. "It's now time for the Silent Auction. Please make your way to the display tables and loosen your purse strings. And remember, it's all for a good cause."

"You're sure you don't want your cake," Max said.

She shook her head. "Thanks, no. I'm curious what they've put up for auction."

He nodded and stood, pulling her chair back for her to rise. "Pick a couple things you like and make a bid on my behalf."

"Oh, I couldn't do that."

"Why not? It's for charity."

"Yes, but—" She broke off. "It wouldn't feel right."

He gave a heavy sigh. "Then pick out something I can donate to a good cause."

She liked that idea much better. "That could be fun."

With the exception of several interruptions, Max actually enjoyed himself during the next hour. Lilli's careful assessment of the items amused him. He noticed she spent an inordinate amount of time studying an expensive baby stroller before she dismissed it and moved along.

"Which should I buy to give away?" he asked, curious what her answer would be.

"The spa and makeover packages for the women's shelter downtown. The deluxe computer system for the homeless shelter."

"That's all?"

"I think they'll provide good bang for the buck."

"You didn't see anything you like? Jewelry? A luxury cruise?"

She shook her head and he continued. "Baby stroller."

She gave a start then shook her head again. "That thing costs almost as much as a car. Crazy expensive."

Max couldn't help wondering how long her attitude would last if she were exposed to luxury all the time. In his experience, women tended to easily grow accustomed to the finer things. She amused him at the same time that she attracted him. Her laughter affected him like a strong jolt of java and her determination not to brown-nose him startled him. He was surrounded by yes people and she didn't hesitate to tell him no. Even though she was pregnant, or perhaps partly because of it, she drew his attention the way no other woman had.

How could she possibly be so innocent and sexy at the same time? He couldn't believe his half brother's damn good luck in finding her. She couldn't be perfect, though, he reminded himself. No one was, and he'd never met a woman who didn't have the capacity for deceit and manipulation. Still, he wanted her. And he wasn't inclined to resist her.

Seven

"You absolutely shouldn't have gotten that baby stroller," Lilli said in a huffy voice. "It was insanely expensive."

"Butter bean will like it," Max said.

She threw him a sideways glance as he opened the door to the house for her. "He would have been just as happy with a less costly model."

"You don't know that," Max argued. "The cutting-edge aerodynamic design, which features an unparalleled smooth ride," he quoted from the manufacturer, "may make a huge difference."

"In that case, he'd better be flexible because my compact car gives a high five to every bump in the road."

He chuckled.

She turned to face him. "But seriously, I cannot accept the jewelry."

"It's just sterling silver."

"David Yurman's top-of-the-line." She shook her head. "I don't understand why you bought it for me. I told you I didn't want anything."

"I'm sure that was part of it," he said.

"You mean you gave me this just to be disagreeable?" she asked, her eyes rounding in surprise.

"It contributed, plus as the hostess kept saying, it's all for charity."

Her lips twitched. "You don't believe any of it. You don't believe the manufacturer's brag about the stroller and you think it's stupid to hold an auction to get donations."

"It's a lot easier to just guilt people into giving money through the mail," he said.

"But for some people, it's more fun to give it away at an auction."

He nodded. "Depends on the people."

She bit her lip and her expression changed. "Maybe." She paused. "I still don't understand why you got me the jewelry."

"The blue topaz reminded me of your eyes," he said.

He saw a hint of something deeper than desire flash through her eyes before she took a quick breath and looked away. "Oh."

His gut twisted with a surprising instinct to pull her against him and kiss her. Take her. He swore under his breath.

She cleared her throat. "Well, you shouldn't have, but it was very nice of you."

"I surprised you," he said. "You thought I was a selfish miser like Scrooge."

"I never thought you were like Scrooge." She paused and seemed to decide that she shouldn't elaborate.

He would love to know what she was really thinking.

"Thank you again. I should go up to bed," she said and paused. "I was wondering," she began and abruptly stopped.

"Wondering what?"

"It's really none of my business."

"I won't know if that's true until you ask the question."

"I was wondering," she ventured. "Do you have any godchildren?"

He narrowed his eyes. "Why do you ask? Did someone mention that to you tonight?"

"At the auction?" she said. "Of course not."

He tugged at his tie. "The truth is I have five godchildren."

Her eyes rounded. "Omigoodness. So many."

He waved his hand in a dismissive gesture. "I'm not expected to do any real parenting. I'm actually a co-godparent. The parents just want my financial management in case anything should happen to them. Along with the gifts and tuition," he added.

"Gifts and tuition?" she echoed, her brow furrowing in confusion.

"They're counting on me to provide a significant college fund."

"For five children?" she said. "Isn't that a bit much?"

"I've got it," he said. "But I've started dodging the opportunity to add any more godchildren."

"I can't blame you for that. My goodness, no wonder you're so cynical."

"No need for flattery," he said, chuckling at her assessment.

Her gaze softened. "But it is very generous of you to accept the responsibility."

"Financial responsibility," he corrected.

She gave a slow nod. "Whatever would you do if, for some unforeseen reason, you became the guardian of five children?"

"Boarding school," he said.

Her face fell. "Oh. That's why I'll never sign your agreement for butter bean."

"You don't really have anyone in mind to be the guardian for your child, do you?" he asked.

She looked away. "I really am working on it."

He touched her arm. "Lilli, tell me the truth."

She bit her lip. "The closest I have is my good friend Dee. She's loving and affectionate and adores children. But she's also a free spirit and loves to travel." She sighed and lifted her lips in a smile that didn't reach her eyes. "Maybe I should place a want ad."

"Never," he said.

"That's what I have to say about boarding school," she replied. The silence hung between them, thick with pent-up desire and emotion. It was so strong he could taste it.

"I should go to bed. Thank you again for an amazing evening. Good night," she said and turned to go upstairs.

He felt the same twitchy sensation he'd felt the first time he'd met her. It was the same feeling of intuition he had just before he made a successful business move. He'd never felt it about a woman, he thought, shaking his head. Loosening his tie, he picked up the weekend edition of one of his newspapers and sat down for a few minutes.

Restless, he decided to pour a glass of red wine. Taking it outside on the patio, he inhaled the scent of the flowers his gardener kept in meticulous condition year-round and listened to the soothing sound of the waterfall in the pool.

Max wondered what would have happened between him and Lilli if they'd met under different circumstances. If she'd never been involved with his brother and gotten pregnant. For just a moment, he indulged himself. He would have seduced her immediately. He would have talked her into quitting her job so she could travel with him at a moment's notice.

The image of her pale naked body available to him at all times made him hard. She was a passionate woman and he would want to learn all of her secrets. He would find out what made her moan, what made her sweat and what would make her come alive in his arms.

He would want to mark her as his with jewelry, but not marriage. Although he'd never invited a woman to live in his home, Lilli may very well have been the first.

Of course, he would have asked her to sign a financial agreement that would protect both her and him for the time when their relationship ended. Every good thing came to an end, Max knew that. He suspected she would have refused to sign the agreement, he thought with a twinge of humor, and he would have had the affair with her anyway.

He swallowed a drink of wine and ruthlessly cut off

his little mental fantasy. With the impending birth of his brother's child, there was far more at stake than Max's libido. Even though he was encouraged by how seriously Lilli was taking her maternal duties, he knew that attitude could change for a variety of reasons.

His own brother's guardian had started out well, but when Tony had hit his teens, the guardian had seemed to give up. She'd allowed Tony way too much freedom and Max was convinced the lack of parental influence had sent Tony down the road into trouble and eventually to his death.

Max refused to allow that to happen to another De Luca. If Lilli continued to refuse to sign an agreement with him, there were other ways. More drastic, more costly, but perhaps ultimately necessary.

Two days later, Lilli left work a little early because Max had invited her to join him for dinner at The Trillion Resort's rooftop restaurant. His assistant had made the arrangements with her, and she had no idea why he'd invited her. Since the auction, Max had worked such late hours she hadn't seen him at all.

She fussed over what to wear and finally chose a pair of maternity slacks and a silk top with varying colors of sea-blue that featured an Empire waist and fell nearly to her knees.

She wore the sterling jewelry Max had purchased for her at the auction and had gone a little more daring with her makeup by giving her eyes a smoky look.

Although she cursed herself for it, she wanted to look nice for Max. She rolled her eyes at the way she minimized her feelings. The truth was she wanted to make his head spin. It was only fair since the man could turn her upside down with just a glance.

Max's chauffeur drove her in one of the luxury sedans. As he pulled in front of the palatial resort, a valet rushed to her door to open it. "Good evening. Mr. De Luca's guest?"

She nodded in surprise as she accepted his assistance out of the car. "Yes, how did you—"

The young man smiled. "We know all of Mr. De Luca's vehicles."

"Oh," she said, nodding. "Thank you." She turned back to Max's chauffeur, Ricardo. "Thank you for the ride."

Ricardo smiled at her and waved. "My pleasure, Miss McCall. Enjoy your evening."

Lilli made her way to the glass elevators that whisked her up to the top level of the resort. Walking into the restaurant, she looked for Max. A man beside her said, "May I help…"

Her gaze collided with Max's across the room and she didn't hear anything else. He rose from the table where he sat, his gaze fixed on her.

The intensity with which he watched her made her feel as if she couldn't breathe. Her heart felt as if it were tripping over itself. Why did this man affect her on so many levels?

She walked to his table and he extended his hand, taking hers. "You look beautiful."

"Thank you," she whispered and took a shallow breath. "This is lovely."

"I thought you might enjoy a night out," he said and glanced down at the necklace she wore. He touched the pendant and his warm fingers brushed her bare skin. "I like the way my gift looks on you."

The hint of sensual possessiveness in his tone gave her a surprising, forbidden thrill. She was a liberated woman. For Pete's sake, what was wrong with her?

"Have a seat," he said before she could reply. "I already ordered orange juice and seltzer for you."

"Thank you." She sat down and felt the hum of anticipation and electricity wind a little tighter between them.

The waiter appeared at their table, offered suggestions and they placed their orders. Max was all charming conversation, pointing out different sights from the restaurant's breathtaking view as the sun slid lower on the horizon.

Tonight interruptions were kept to a minimum. Although Lilli felt plenty of gazes on her and Max, no one approached the table. The waitstaff were perfect, appearing to refill drinks, clear plates and provide nearly invisible but courteous service.

"I told the maître' d I wanted as few interruptions as possible tonight," Max said as if he'd read her mind.

She nodded. "I couldn't help comparing this experience to the auction."

"The auction was a free-for-all. Now you understand why I don't attend many," he said and lifted his hand. "Although I must say I enjoyed it much more because you were there."

"It was fun and I made a new friend," she said.

"Who?"

"Mallory James. She invited me to lunch on Saturday."

He nodded his head in approval. "Good. You'll be occupied."

Strange response, she thought. "Occupied for what?"

"I'm going out of town for three weeks."

Her heart sank. Crazy. She would have to think about that later. "Oh, wow. That's a long trip."

"Yes. I knew it was coming. We have several grand reopenings in different locations scheduled over the next few weeks and my presence is required at all of them."

"The bane of being the boss," she said, forcing a smile because, heaven help her, she would miss him.

"These arrangements were made before I knew you existed. I'll be out of the country," he said, clearly displeased. "I'm not comfortable leaving you at this stage."

His confession made her feel as if the sun came out from behind a cloud. "I've got six weeks until my due date. Everything's been perfect so far. There's no reason to think I'll have any problems."

"Still," he said. "It's best to be prepared for everything. Give me your cell phone."

She blinked. "Why?"

"So I can program in my contact numbers," he said.

"Oh, I can't imagine that I would need to call you while you're out of the country," she said.

He waved his fingers impatiently and she gave him her phone. "Of course, you'll be talking to me. I'll be checking in with you on a regular basis. For any immediate emergencies, you're to call my assistant, Grace. I've told her to be on twenty-four hour call."

"That's ridiculous. I wouldn't call your assistant. I've never even met her."

"If you're not comfortable, I can arrange a meeting."

Overwhelmed, Lilli shook her head. "No. That's not

necessary." She lowered her voice. "None of this is necessary. I'll be fine."

He met her gaze. "It's my job to make sure you
stay that way."

"Why?" she demanded. "It's not as if you're my
hus—" She broke off, horrified that the words had just
popped out of her mouth.

Unable to tear her gaze from his, Lilli felt something
snap and shimmer between them. A forbidden possibility
neither of them would consider. What if Max *was* her
husband? What if… Feeling as if the circuits in her head
had scrambled and misfired, she looked away from him.

She took a mind-clearing breath. "That was stupid.
This is about the baby. You feel responsible because
you're the uncle. It's not about me."

He cleared his throat. "It's all connected. The baby,
you, me. And since your delivery date is growing closer,
you must make a decision about guardianship if something should happen to you."

She glanced back at him and watched him pull a
manila envelope from his suit jacket pocket. "I've asked
my attorney to come up with an agreement that should
be more palatable for you. While I'm gone, I want you
to look at this and take it to another attorney if that will
make you more comfortable."

Her heart twisted. This entire meal had been a setup.
Max wanted one thing and one thing alone from her.
Control of her baby. Although she wanted to toss the
agreement back at him, she felt forced to take the
envelope for the sake of civility.

Max seemed to sense the change in her mood and
signed for the check and escorted her from the dining

room. She hated sharing the close space of the elevator, but getting into the Ferrari with him was far more excruciating. The darkness closed around them, creating a veil of intimacy.

Every time he shifted gears, her gaze strayed to his hand tightening around the knob. His long legs flexed as he accelerated and pushed in the clutch. Despite her hostility, she couldn't help noticing a commanding sensuality with the way he drove the luxury sports car. He would be a commanding, demanding lover, she knew, but he would also make sure his partner was satisfied. In fact, she suspected a woman might never be the same once she'd shared a bed with Max.

As soon as he pulled into the garage and came to a stop, she turned to unlock her door. The second after she hit the button, the automatic lock clicked again, effectively trapping her in the car with Max. Inhaling a shallow breath, she caught a draft of his masculine scent with just a hint of cologne.

Although she fought its effect on her, she couldn't deny feeling light-headed and entirely too aware of him as a man. "What do you want?" she asked without turning to look at him.

"You haven't had a chance to read my attorney's proposal, so you can't be upset about it. But you haven't said a word since we left the restaurant. Why?"

She stiffened her resolve against his gentle, reasonable voice. "You don't seem to understand. My baby is not for sale."

Three seconds of silence passed before she felt his hand on her arm. "Look at me. You can't really believe that I intend to buy your child."

She reluctantly faced him. "Why should I believe anything else? You've been trying to cram money down my throat since the first time I met you. In exchange for control of my child." She willed herself to keep her voice from wavering. "You said I should find this agreement more palatable. You don't seem to understand that it doesn't matter how much money you pile onto the agreement, I'm not giving up my baby to you."

He stared at her in shock. "Is that what you think? That the new agreement is about money? It isn't. It gives you far more rights than the previous one. Good God, do you really think I'm that much of an ogre?"

Glimpsing his sincerity, she bit her lip in confusion. "I didn't know what else to think. You invite me to a fabulous dinner where you act as if you're actually enjoying my company then slap me with a contract."

"Of course I enjoyed dinner with you. Otherwise, I could have left the contract with one of my staff to give to you. And I wanted you to have my contact numbers. This is my last night in town for a while. I wanted to spend it with you."

Her heart hammered against her rib cage and she shook her head. "You're confusing me. I don't know what you want from me," she said. "Other than to sign your agreement."

He looked into her eyes for a long moment then his gaze traveled to her lips and lingered. He lifted his gaze again to hers and she felt scorched by the desire she saw there.

"You want to know what I want from you?" he asked in a low voice. Then he lowered his head and took her mouth. He slid one of his hands under her jaw and cupped her face as if she were both precious and sensuous. The gesture undid her.

He devoured her mouth in dizzying kisses as he gently rubbed his hands down her neck, massaging her taut muscles.

His kiss turned her body into a bow of tension, eager for him. His massaging fingers gentled her, clouding her mind, making her willing to do whatever he wanted.

His mouth continued to take hers while his fingers drifted across her collarbone and lower to the tops of her breasts. She felt her nipples strain against the cups of her bra. Restlessness and need swelled inside her.

He paused a half beat then slid his fingertips beneath the top of her blouse, brushing them over her sensitized nipples. She gasped in pleasure at the sensation.

He pulled his hands from her breasts and placed them on her shoulders. He pulled his mouth a breath away from hers and it was all she could do to keep from asking him not to stop.

"I want you," he said against her mouth. "I want you in every way you can imagine and probably a few you can't. But now is not the time." He slid one of his hands through her hair. "Promise me that you'll take care of yourself while I'm away. No taking chances. And call me if you need me."

Lilli closed her eyes. She'd felt the power of his desire. What frightened her was the fact that her desire for him matched his. What frightened her even more was the very real possibility that she could need Max in ways *he* would never dream.

Eight

Two and a half weeks later, Lilli dragged herself from her little car up the steps from the mansion's garage. Her back and legs had been aching all day. She felt tired and cranky and, heaven help her, she missed Max. He called frequently, and every time, she felt the tension between them twist a little tighter.

She'd spent more than one night flirting with the forbidden fantasy of Max being the father of her child. Right now, though, all she wanted to focus on was getting a sandwich, taking a shower and going to bed.

Stepping into the foyer, she stopped and drank in a moment of peace and quiet then walked toward the kitchen.

"Surprise!" a chorus of voices called, startling her so much she dropped her water bottle and purse.

Her friends clapped in delight.

"We did it," her best friend Dee crowed. "We surprised you."

"Yes, you did." Lilli felt some of her weariness fade away and smiled. "How did you pull this off?"

"Because we're your brilliant friends, of course," Dee said. "And I think Mallory here has a magic wand. She knew how to deal with the staff, and just wait until you see the cake she brought."

"Cake?" Lilli echoed and gave Mallory a hug as the woman walked toward her. She'd enjoyed a few lunches with Mallory during the last two weeks and Lilli already had a soft spot for the woman. "You shouldn't have."

"It's nothing. I'm just glad to be a part of all this. Now come in and sit down. Let me get you some sherbet punch."

After Lilli opened the gifts for her and the baby, Mallory presented Lilli with a large sheet cake decorated with a baby in a blue buggy inscribed with frosted letters, "Happy Baby, Lilli!" The cake was lit with one candle.

"Make a wish and blow out the candle," Mallory said.

"But it's not my birthday."

"It's your first baby. You can add more candles when you have more babies."

Lilli looked at her in horror. "More?"

"Okay, let's just focus on one, then," Mallory quickly amended. "Make a wish and blow out the candle."

Lilli closed her eyes and wished for a safe and easy delivery and good health for her baby. Secretly, she wished for a father for her child. An image of the man she would choose appeared in her mind. She blinked, pushing aside the thought. Crazy and impossible, she thought. Must be the hormones.

Just after she opened the last gift, the room abruptly turned silent.

"Major hot guy alert," Dee whispered.

Lilli turned to see Max standing in the doorway, a wrapped package in his hand. "Max," she said, stunned. "I thought you were still traveling."

"I just got back thirty minutes ago. You didn't tell me you were having a baby shower," he said in a lightly chastising tone.

Lilli drank in the sight of him. Holding her breath, she wondered if he had looked forward to seeing her again as much as she had looked forward to having him back home. She wondered if he still wanted her the same way he had before.

Dee cleared her throat. "It was a surprise shower," she said to Max. "What's in the box?"

He gave a brief glance to Dee then moved toward Lilli. His gaze dipped to her belly.

"I've gotten bigger," she said, unable to keep herself from smiling.

He gave a half grin. "So you have. And still glowing." He gave her the small but beautifully wrapped box. "Myrtle left a message for me about the shower. I thought you could use this."

Her hands trembled and she wished they would stop. She hadn't seen Max in weeks and she would just like to sit down and talk with him. She managed to open the box and found a gift certificate inside. "One mother's helper of your choice from Personalized Nanny Services for one year."

Mallory nodded in approval. "PNS is the very best."

"A nanny?" Lilli said, staring at Max. "I hadn't planned—"

"Oh, no," Dee said. "You're not turning this one down. She loves it," Dee said to Max. "Perfect gift. Thank you very much." She turned back to Lilli. "If you get tired of having her around, you can send her over to my place. I would love for someone to make peanut butter and jelly sandwiches and chocolate chip cookies for me."

Several of the women moaned in agreement. "Will she do laundry? Will she grocery shop?"

Max met Lilli's gaze. "She'll do whatever Lilli wants her to do."

There was another group moan followed by a collective sigh.

"Can I see you privately for a moment?" he asked.

Lilli felt a combination kick from the baby and a flutter from her heart. "Sure," she said, rising from her seat.

"Ask him about Alex," Mallory whispered.

Tearing her gaze from Max, she glanced at Mallory. "Ask him what about Alex?"

"Where he hangs out after work. I introduced him to my father and haven't seen him since."

"From what Max says, that could be for the best. Alex is supposed to be a major player."

"I'd just like the opportunity to find out for myself," Mallory said.

"Okay. I'll see what I can do," she said, but her mind wasn't on Alex or Mallory. It was dominated by Max.

She followed him into the foyer, noticing subtle changes in his appearance. His hair was just a little longer, more wavy. When he turned to face her, she noticed his eyes looked a bit weary as he studied her.

"It's a nice surprise to see you," she said. "I had no idea you'd be back so soon."

"I'm glad I could make it. Are you okay? Any of Tony's friends hanging around?"

"I'm fine and I haven't seen any of Tony's friends in a long time."

"Good," he said and held her gaze. "I have another event I'm expected to attend tonight, but we need to talk sometime soon. Have you looked over the agreement I left with you?"

She felt a rush of disappointment. "Yes, I have."

"Good," he said again. His gaze seemed to say so much more, but Lilli wondered if she was imagining it. "I won't keep you from your friends."

She felt another twist of disappointment. That was it. No *I'm glad to see you, I want you...* Nothing. She stared, waiting, wanting.

"Good night," he said and turned toward the door.

Lilli continued to stare after him, starting to feel like a fool. Had she misunderstood? "Wait," she said.

He stopped just as he reached the door and turned around. "Yes?"

Her heart raced. Confused, she didn't know what to say. "I...uh..." She groped for something to say. "Mallory asked me to ask you about Alex."

"Alex Megalos?" he said with a frown, walking back toward her.

"Yes. I think she'd like to get to know him better. She

was wondering where he usually hangs out after work," she said, suddenly feeling like a middle schooler.

He shook his head. "I have no idea."

She gave a slow nod. "Okay" she said. "I'll tell her."

He shrugged. "I can probably find out something from my assistant."

"Thanks." She hesitated a half beat, hating the awkwardness between them. "Are you okay?"

"Yeah. Just tired and harassed. I've been on longer trips, but this one felt like it went on forever."

She nodded again. "Yeah, it did—" She broke off before she added *for me, too*. Feeling her cheeks heat from his knowing gaze, she cleared her throat. "Why do you think it felt so long?"

"I think you know," he said and moved closer to her.

"You want me to sign the agreement about the baby," she said in a husky voice.

"That's part of it." He lowered his head. He inhaled sharply and closed his eyes then stepped back. God help him, if he started kissing her, he wouldn't stop. Being away from her hadn't cleared his perspective or dampened his desire for her. And Max knew there wasn't a damn thing he could do about wanting her at the moment. He'd missed the sound of her laughter and knowing she would be there at home for the end of the day.

Maybe it was a good thing he had to attend the charity fund-raiser tonight after all. Being with Lilli was a constant reminder of what he couldn't have.

"I should go," he said in a low voice. "We can talk more on Friday. Tomorrow will be a busy day."

"Okay, thank you for the gift."

"You're welcome," he said and held her gaze for a long moment before he left.

The following evening, Lilli flipped through the newspaper as she put up her feet at the end of a long day. She glanced at the bad news on the front page, skipped the Sports section and stopped at the Life-style section. The front page featured photos of a charity function sponsored by Max's company. In one of the photos, Kiki stood next to Max, her arm looped through his. He didn't look as if he were suffering at all.

A surge of something dark twisted through her and when she realized what it was, she felt more stupid than ever. She was jealous. Maybe it was hormones. Oh Lord, she hoped so. Because if it were hormones then at some point, when her hormones straightened out again, the crazy longing would go away.

Restless after reading the article, she took a long bath and listened to soothing music. She sipped herbal tea to calm herself and tried not to think about that photo of Max with Kiki.

She slept horribly, unable to get comfortable. Giving up on sleep, she rose earlier than usual. When she got out of bed, she felt exhausted and noticed her abdomen tightening. As she prepared for work, the sensation didn't go away. Were these contractions?

Although she had a few weeks left before her due date she called her doctor's office. The doctor on call asked a few questions then, erring on the cautious side, instructed her to go to the hospital.

Lilli grabbed her purse and went downstairs. Max

stood poised to leave. He met her gaze. "Good morning. How are you?"

Lilli burst into tears.

Alarmed by her response, Max dropped his briefcase and immediately took her in her arms. "What is it? What's wrong?"

She choked back a sob. "I may be in labor. My doctor told me to go to the hospital. Max, this is happening too fast." Her blue eyes filled with tears of desperation. "I'm not ready."

"Of course you are," he said firmly even though his own gut was clenching in apprehension. "I'll drive you to the hospital and—"

"Are you sure that's what you want—?"

"Of course I'm sure," he said, appalled that she would expect anything less of him. "We'll take the town car." He ushered her to the garage. "I'll drive. You can sit in the backseat and stretch out."

His own heart hammering in his chest, Max helped her into the car and sped to the hospital. He shot a glance at Lilli in the rearview mirror and the expression of fear on her face tore at him. "You're going to be okay. The baby is going to be okay."

"Do you really believe that?"

He nodded. "Yes, I do." He had to believe it.

Pulling the car to a stop outside the emergency room door, he helped Lilli inside. An admission clerk took her information and Lilli was whisked away. Just before she disappeared behind the double doors, she looked back at Max. "Are you leaving?"

He shook his head. "I'll be right back after I park the car." Returning to the hospital, he was consumed with concern for Lilli and the baby. He would get the finest doctors in Las Vegas to care for her. He would do whatever it took to keep Lilli and the baby safe and healthy.

He strode toward the emergency room double doors, making a mental list. A woman stepped in front of him. "Excuse me, sir. You're not allowed inside unless you're a member of a patient's family."

Frustration ripped through him. He needed to take care of Lilli, but it wasn't his official duty or his official right. At that moment, he made a life-altering decision. He knew there would be no going back. But never again would he worry about being barred from taking care of Lilli or the baby. He would make her his wife. That way, taking care of her and the baby would always be his right. "I'm the baby's father," he told the woman, and she allowed him to pass.

Two and a half hours later, a mortified Lilli left the hospital with Max. "I'm so sorry," she said, shooting a wincing glance at him. His hair was ruffled from plowing his fingers through it and his tie hung loose from his collar. He was more gorgeous than ever and she felt like a lunatic. "I should have realized it was false labor."

"Like the doctor said, it's an easy mistake to make. This is your first pregnancy."

"Maybe," she said. "But now you've lost half a day of work because of my mistake."

"A half day of work is nothing to make sure you and the baby are safe," he said, his words barely softening the harsh sound of his voice as he drove them home. "Stop apologizing."

She bit her lip and looked out the window then back at him. "Are you sure you're not angry?"

"I'm not angry, but I am concerned. This under-scores the need for you to provide for the baby if something, God forbid, should happen to you," he said and swore under his breath.

"I know," she said glumly. She knew she couldn't dodge it any longer. "I'm going to change my will today so that you'll be the baby's guardian."

He narrowed his eyes at her words. "That's a good start, but we may need to take that further."

Her chest tightened. He was talking about the agreement he wanted her to sign. Even though she understood the money in the agreement was designated for support, she still found it distasteful. "I don't want your money and I don't want to sign the agreement. It just feels totally wrong to me."

"I'm not talking about that agreement," he said, pulling the car into a bank parking lot and cutting the engine.

Lilli looked at him in surprise. "Then what?"

"I've been thinking. How do you feel about the baby's last name being De Luca?"

She frowned in confusion. "I thought I was going to try not to draw attention to the fact that Tony was his father. For safety's sake. That's the reason I'll be moving away."

"What if you didn't move away?" he asked, his gaze searching hers. "What if your last name became De Luca, too?"

More confused than ever, she shook her head. "How could that happen?"

"If you named me the father of—" he paused "—your child. And married me."

She gaped at him, feeling as if someone had turned the whole world upside down. "Married you? But you don't love me."

"Starting out in love isn't the best predictor of success in marriage."

Her head was whirling. "I don't understand. You don't want to get married. You're pretty cynical about marriage."

"I want to provide a good life for the baby. I feel responsible for him. For you," he said as if he didn't totally understand his own feelings.

"I don't think that's a good basis for a marriage."

"There's a lot worse," he said.

Her chest tightened. "I don't want to feel like a responsibility. Like a burden. And I don't want the baby to ever feel that way."

"It *wouldn't* be that way. I think you and I could make this work." He slid his hand under her jaw. "And there's the fact that I want you. And you want me," he said, his tone intimate.

"I wondered if maybe that had changed."

He slowly shook his head.

Her heart skipped over itself. "What about when that does change?"

"How do you know it will?" he asked, his dark eyes holding hers.

Lilli felt herself sinking into a delicious, forbidden pool of hope. "I don't know."

He caressed her jaw. "I think you know that you and I would be good together. In a lot of ways."

True. But that didn't mean they should get married. Lilli tore away her gaze to clear her head. If she put the baby's needs in front of hers, what would she do? She felt an immediate smack from her conscience. Who was she fooling? It wasn't as if being with Max De Luca would present a hardship for her. But this was a huge decision. Huge enough that she wanted to make it with a clear head.

"Could you give me some time to think this over?"

He met her gaze and nodded. "Sure." He paused a half beat. "Think about it. You'll realize it's best for everyone."

She felt a sliver of relief. She'd bought herself a little time.

"Do you have any questions you'd like to ask me?" he said, as if he sensed what was going on inside her.

She closed her eyes so she wouldn't be affected by his presence, but she still sensed him, still smelled the faintest scent of his sexy cologne. "If you raised the baby, would you blow bubbles with him?"

He didn't even pause. "Yes."

"Will you read him books at night? You can let the nanny do it every now and then, but you need to do it most nights."

"Yes," he said.

"Will you tell him he's wonderful?"

"Yes."

"Will you hold him when he cries?"

"Yes. And I'll hold you, too, Lilli, whether you're crying or not."

And Lilli felt her heart tumble a little farther away from good sense and sanity.

Nine

"I like it," Max said to Alex during a one-on-one meeting in his office. "At first glance, when you say West Virginia, I would think the local economy wouldn't be able to support this kind of luxury resort."

Alex tapped his pen on his outline. "Because it's close to Washington, D.C., there's great transportation access. D.C. residents will be rushing there every weekend."

"The sticking point with the board will be the mid-week challenge," Max said. "Who wants to go to West Virginia in the middle of the week?"

"We can hold meetings and conferences. Plus, if we do it right, this place will have a spa, golf course, special events and all kinds of luxury amenities that will draw people year-round."

"Like I said, I like it. You've got my—" His intercom

beeped, interrupting him. Surprised because he'd told his assistant no interruptions during his meeting, he picked up his phone. "Yes."

"I'm terribly sorry to interrupt you, Mr. De Luca, but security downstairs has called and they said a very pregnant woman insists on seeing you."

There was only one very pregnant woman in his life. Immediately concerned, he frowned. "Lilli," he said. "Is she okay?"

His assistant, Grace, made a sound between a cough and swallowed laughter. "She sounds quite healthy, sir. Just very determined to see you. Security was unsure what to do with her."

He nodded, feeling a twinge of amusement at the notion of the beefy guys downstairs trying to handle a demanding pregnant woman. "Send her up immediately."

Alex stood, lifting his eyebrow. "Does this mean our meeting is over?"

"For now," Max said. "Let's set up a time to discuss a strategy for approaching the board about this."

Alex extended his hand. "Sounds great." He gathered his report and headed for the office door. Just as he reached for it, the door flung open and Lilli burst inside. Her cheeks bright red, she carried a large rectangular plastic food container.

"Good grief," she said. "Do you train your security to suspect that every pregnant woman is a nut or did I just get lucky today?"

Max chuckled under his breath and moved toward her to take the container. "It won't happen again. Here, let me help—"

"No," Alex said and grabbed the container before

Max could. "Allow me and let me say you look gorgeous as ever."

Flirting again, Max thought with more than a pinch of irritation. Did the man ever stop?

"I look like a blond beach ball," she told Alex. "But thanks for the effort. Would you do me a favor and call a few of the assistants into the office?"

Max frowned. "What—"

"Sure," Alex said and set the container down on a table.

Lilli smiled nervously as she met Max's gaze. "This won't take but a few minutes. Then you can get back to whatever you were doing."

Max shook his head. "But what is *this?*"

She gnawed her lip. "Just a little something."

Her expression made him uneasy. *What the...*

Alex reappeared in the doorway with several members of the staff, their faces filled with curiosity. "Ready for service," Alex said.

"Thank you," Lilli said and went to the table where the plastic container sat. "I just need to borrow your voices for two minutes. Today is Max's birthday, so I was hoping you would join with me in singing 'Happy Birthday.'" She whipped off the top of the container to reveal a collection of frosted cupcakes decorated with sprinkles. "Sorry you can't blow out the candles," she said with a moue. "Security took my matches. Okay, let's go."

Max stood in stunned disbelief as she led the small group in song. Alex laughed the entire way through the tune.

When they finished, Lilli shot him a wary glance and a tentative smile. "Happy Birthday, Max."

Max met her gaze and felt his heart swell to at least twice its normal size. He hadn't celebrated his birthday in years. It was just another day to him. "How did you know?"

"That's a secret," she said. "But I didn't know your favorite kind of cupcake, so I made a variety. Vanilla with chocolate frosting, chocolate with chocolate frosting, chocolate with vanilla—"

Alex extended his hand into the container. "I'll take the chocolate with—"

Lilli lightly swatted his hand. "It's Max's birthday. He gets to choose first." She glanced at Max. "What kind do you want?"

I want Lilli with Lilli frosting, he thought and cleared his throat. "Chocolate and chocolate," he said and nodded toward the staff. "Go ahead, help yourself."

Each of his employees took their treats and wished him a happy birthday before they left. Alex lingered an extra moment. "For your information, my birthday is November 16 and I love cupcakes."

Max felt a surge of possessiveness. "Call a bakery," he growled.

Alex laughed and shook his head. "You're a damn lucky man, Max. Happy birthday," he said and left the office.

Closing the door, Max turned toward Lilli, who was sitting in a chair across from his desk, biting off the top of a chocolate cupcake. He walked to the chair across from hers and sat down. "What possessed you to do this?"

"You're not angry, are you?"

He shook his head. "Off guard. Surprised." And a

few other things he didn't want to name. "You didn't answer my question."

She licked her lips and he wished he could do it for her. "It occurred to me that you may not have celebrated your birthday very much when you were in boarding school. That was a bad habit to start at such a young age," she said in a chastising voice that made his lips twitch. "So I thought I should get you back on track."

"Why?"

She met his gaze and he saw a flash of deep emotion shimmer in her eyes. Max could identify things that held a high value and what he saw in her gaze was more precious than all the gems in the exclusive jewelry store down the street.

"I think you are an amazing man. So the day you were born should be celebrated."

Her simple explanation held no false flattery. He heard the sincerity in her voice, saw it on her face, and it was the most seductive thing anyone had ever said to him. Lilli, pregnant or not, made him hungry for more of her. Standing, he took her hand and pulled her close. "Marry me."

He saw the desire and fear collide in her gaze. "It's right," he said. "For all of us."

"How can you be so sure?" she whispered.

"Be honest, Lilli. Underneath it all, you want it, too."

She closed her eyes for a long moment and he could feel her heart hammering against him. She took a small shallow breath and opened her eyes. "Yes, I'll marry you."

Max made the arrangements so quickly Lilli barely had time to catch her breath, let alone her sanity. Three days before he'd scheduled a private wedding ceremony with a judge who was a friend, he and Lilli shared late-night conversation on the patio.

"I picked this up today. Let me know if you like it." He casually slid a box across the table toward her.

Curious, she opened the box. Shocked at the diamond ring winking back at her from the velvet fold of the box, she choked on the water she had just swallowed.

Max patted her on her back. "Are you okay?"

She coughed, tears coming to her eyes, then waved her hand. "Yes." She coughed again and shook her head. "I didn't expect an engagement ring."

"Of course I'd get you a ring."

She stared at the ring, almost afraid to touch it. "The stone is huge."

He was silent for a moment then laughed under his breath. "You're complaining about a large diamond?" he asked in disbelief. "That's a first."

"I'm not complaining," she quickly said. "I just didn't expect it. When I think about us getting married, I haven't thought about diamonds, or even rings."

"Then what have you been thinking?"

She bit her lip, reluctant to reveal the fact that she was wondering if it was such a smart thing to marry Max. She shrugged, not meeting his gaze. "More about how all three of us will adjust to family life." She hesitated. "Wondering how you and I will adjust to being married."

"I think we've demonstrated we won't have any problems," he said, sliding his hands over her neck, making her feel as if her collarbone was a sensual hot spot for the first time in her life. It amazed her that he could make her feel so sexy with just a touch.

She closed her eyes for a second. "In bed," she said in a voice that sounded small to her own ears.

His hands stilled. "What do you mean?"

"Well, it may be a rumor," she said, trying to keep a light tone, "but I hear married couples tend to spend a lot more time out of bed than in bed."

"Damn," he said. "So you may actually have to join me for dinner most nights and we'll have to do things together." He walked around her chair and bent down over her, meeting her gaze. "Sounds rough, but I think I can do it. What about you?"

She smiled reluctantly. "Probably," she said.

"But you're still bothered."

"You have to admit this isn't the typical romantic wedding. We don't even have a honeymoon planned. For that matter, how did you find out my ring size? I didn't know yours."

"While you were sleeping," he said and added, "in your bed. Say what you want, but sex between us will take away a lot of your doubts."

The notion filled her with a combination of anticipation and anxiety. Would she have any leftover reactions to that last experience with Tony? So far, Max seemed to push everything from her mind, but him.

"So try on the ring. Maybe you'll like it better on your finger," he said casually and plucked the ring from the box and slid it onto her hand.

It fit perfectly. It sparkled like a bright star. "It's beautiful," she said and wiggled her finger. "Does it come with a crane?"

* * *

Lilli woke up the next morning full of anticipation and hope. She was just two weeks from her delivery date, two weeks from when she would hold her baby in her arms. The excitement inside her seemed to build with each passing hour. And she was getting married in just two days.

Glancing at the diamond ring that felt heavy on her finger, she fought the slivers of trepidation that stabbed at her. She felt as if she were on the precipice of falling completely in love with Max. What if she spent a lifetime waiting for him to love her and he never did? What if he fell out of lust with her and left her? Or worse yet, what if he never allowed himself to love her, but stayed with her even though he was miserable?

Lilli shook off the thoughts. She had every reason to hope everything would work out well. The sun shining brightly outside seemed to invite her to take a short stroll along the driveway that led to Max's home and then down the block. The fresh air cleared her head and the sunshine gave her a boost of optimism.

Returning from the stroll, she spotted a car parked in the driveway. It was a Jaguar, so she knew it didn't belong to any of her friends. Mallory drove a BMW.

Curious, Lilli entered the house and overheard a woman talking with Ada, the assistant housekeeper. "I left some of my things here several months ago. I just want to pick them up."

Recognizing the woman's voice as Kiki, Lilli stiffened. She turned away to quietly climb the stairs. She didn't want a confrontation with the woman.

"Oh, look, the sweet mother-to-be. Don't run off. It's been too long. We should visit for a little bit," Kiki said.

Lilli reluctantly stopped and turned. "Hello, Kiki."

Looking as svelte and perfect as ever in a fashionable black-and-white sheath, Kiki moved past the housekeeper. "Omigoodness, you look like you're ready to go any minute. Positively glowing," she said. "Babies are pure magic, aren't they? They make the impossible seem possible. I mean, look at how your life has changed."

"I just want what's best for my baby," Lilli said.

"Of course you do," Kiki said. "I was surprised that I never heard back from you after we met at the charity auction. Did you lose my card?"

"Yes. I think I did," Lilli said.

"You seem like a smart woman. I thought you might take me up on my offer. But rumor has it you're placing your bets somewhere else."

Lilli and Max hadn't announced their decision to marry, so Lilli refused to confirm or deny any implications. "I should go upstairs. I have a doctor's appointment this afternoon."

"You can at least show me the nursery," the other woman said with a fake pout. "I'll go upstairs with you. I need to pick up a few things I left here."

Ada stepped forward. "I'm sorry, Miss Lane, but I'm not sure Mr. De Luca would be comfortable with you going through his private quarters. If you'll wait, I can call him."

Alarm shot across Kiki's face. "That's not necessary. I'll give him a call myself. It's just so awkward to ask a man to return lingerie," she whispered. "But it was

La Perla. One of my favorites," she said with a sigh.
"One of his, too, as I recall. Oh, well. Lovely seeing
you. You can still give me a call if you change your mind
about anything, but don't wait too long."

Watching Kiki leave, Lilli told herself not to trust the
woman. Kiki was clearly desperate and would do anything to get Max back. She shouldn't let the woman
generate any doubts about her decision to marry Max.
Her rebellious mind, though, hung on to Kiki's description of lingerie. She remembered the photo of Max and
Kiki in the newspaper just recently. Perhaps she had
underestimated their relationship.

Ten

Lilli's day went from bad to worse when Max presented her with a prenup agreement late that evening. With the exception of the clause that gave Max custody of the baby if they separated and she was determined to be an unsuitable influence, the prenup was very generous. Financially, anyway.

Lilli slept on the agreement, not wanting to overreact. The day before she was scheduled to marry Max, she rose and looked at her large diamond engagement ring and took it off. In a calm voice completely at odds with the turmoil raging inside her, she called Max and asked him to meet her at the house as soon as possible. He arrived an hour later.

"I'm not going to sign it the way it is," she told him and set the ring and the agreement on the patio table in front of him.

His mouth twisted as he glanced down at the ring and the unsigned agreement. "You want more?"

"No. I'm not going to leave the judgment of my ability to parent up to a court that could be bought or skewed by your influence.

He met her gaze. "It's not money?" He paused a half beat. "Are you sure this isn't about Kiki's offer?"

She couldn't hide her surprise.

He walked toward her, dressed in a suit that emphasized his height, power and attractiveness. "You didn't know that I knew? The housekeeper told me she came to visit. She seemed to imply she'd made some prior offer and I can only imagine it was meant as a buy off."

"Apparently she came by to collect some expensive lingerie she'd left," she said, refusing to give in to his effect on her.

"That was a lie. I've never invited Kiki to stay in my bedroom. Why didn't you tell me that she was trying to buy you off?"

Trying to digest the fact that Kiki's La Perla lingerie had never made it into Max's bedroom, she fought another wave of confusion. "I didn't know if you were still in love with her."

He lifted a dark eyebrow. "I've told you my opinion of romantic love. It doesn't last."

His words cut, but she didn't want to show it. "I didn't feel comfortable telling you. I felt like I should handle her on my own."

"Or maybe you were holding out for a better offer than I gave you in the prenup."

Lilli felt a spurt of anger. "If you really believe that, then we definitely shouldn't get married."

Max met her gaze. "What do you want?"

"Strike the clause about my being an unfit mother."

"Done," he said. "If Kiki contacts you again, you must tell me."

She paused a brief second. "I will," she said. "Are you sure you don't have some leftover feelings for her? She is more beautiful than I am," she impulsively blurted.

He stared at her in surprise. "I disagree."

Perhaps she should have felt affirmed. Instead her insecurities seemed to bubble up from deep inside her. "She knows how to operate in your crowd."

"She's manipulative as hell. Do you really think I want to be married to a woman like that?"

Lilli realized she needed to get her questions answered, or she would be victimized by her doubts forever. She took a deep breath and braced herself. "I think I need to know your stand on fidelity in our marriage. Since this isn't a love match, do you consider yourself free to have—" she forced the word from her tight throat "—affairs?"

His face turned to stone. "Absolutely not. Once we marry, you will be the only woman in my bed and I will be the only man in yours. I take my vows very seriously. If you can't make the same kind of commitment, then you'd better tell me, because I'll expect the same complete fidelity that I'll give."

His fierce response took her breath away. Perhaps she should have known. A man like Max wouldn't make a marital commitment easily and he would not only give, but expect to receive complete loyalty from his wife.

"I can't even imagine being unfaithful to you." What woman would want to?

His expression gentled a millimeter and he picked up the ring. "Then you won't need to take this off ever again," he said and slid the diamond on her finger. "I'm giving you and your baby my name and adopting him. Our marriage will work. I've decided it will," he said. "Understand?"

Even though there was no judge or minister present, at that very moment, she felt as if they were exchanging vows. He was making a promise he would keep and she was doing the same. "Yes, I understand."

The following day, Max arranged for the prenup to be changed. Lilli signed it and put on a cream-colored silk dress with a voluminous amount of material beneath the Empire waist that allowed for her advanced pregnancy. Her stomach jumped with butterflies. She told herself to put aside her fears, but in the back of her mind, although she feared that Max would take his commitments seriously, she knew he might never grow to love her.

A dull nagging ache in her back and those dancing butterflies continued to distract her, but she was determined to be as beautiful a bride for Max as possible. She clipped her hair back in a half up-do and added a fresh pink rose above the clip.

The ceremony was truly private with only the judge and Jim Gregory and Myrtle serving as witnesses. The weather was beautiful as usual and she and Max said their vows on the patio where they'd shared dinner the first night she'd stayed at his house. There was something right about that, something right in knowing they would share many more dinners on the very spot where they'd made lifelong promises to each other.

She told herself not to worry, but her hands were cold with nerves as Max held them.

"I pronounce you husband and wife," the judge said. "You may now kiss the bride."

Max drew her against him and slowly covered her mouth with his in a kiss that echoed the promises they'd just made.

Afterward, they shared a private lunch on the patio, just the two of them and toasted their marriage with sparkling water and orange juice.

"To us and our life together," he said.

She nodded. "To us." She took a long sip then another, her mind reeling with what she'd just done. She'd just married a man who cared for her, but didn't love her.

"You're very quiet."

She nodded again. "It's a big day. A lot to think about," she managed.

"You can relax now. We'll have more to think about after the baby is born. After your recovery."

He was talking about sex, she realized. There would be no night of passion tonight. One more way this day was odd. "The doctor told me that's usually four to six weeks," she said, feeling her cheeks heat.

He covered her hand with his and her heart took an extra beat. "Where would you like to honeymoon? We can go anywhere you like."

"I haven't even thought about it," she said.

He stroked the inside of her wrist. "You should. By the time we go on ours, we will have both earned it. Yes?"

Her chest tightened at the sight of his hand caressing hers. "I guess you're right."

"So tell me where you'd like to go," he said.

She fought a sudden shyness. "Somewhere with a beach?"

He nodded. "The company has resorts all over, but I also have access to some private spots. We would have staff, but no one else around to intrude."

"That sounds nice," she managed. "I wish it could be sooner."

He gave a rough chuckle. "You and me both, sweetheart." He sighed and lifted her hand to his lips. "The anticipation will either kill us or make the experience explosive."

"Or both," she said.

He laughed again. "We should eat."

Her stomach still doing dips and turns, Lilli picked at the meal. Her back was hurting like the dickens. She shifted uncomfortably in her chair.

"Is something bothering you?" he asked.

"I hate to complain, but may back hurts and—" She sighed. "I don't know. Maybe it's the excitement, but I don't feel very hungry at all." She felt a sudden telltale surge of liquid and stared at him startled.

"What is it?"

"I think I'm in labor. Real labor, this time," she added. "I think my water broke."

Her announcement galvanized Max into action. The wide-eyed expression of fear on her face clutched at his gut. He immediately told his driver to start the car and grabbed the suitcase Lilli had packed after her experience with false labor.

Hustling her into the backseat of the town car within three minutes, he slid in beside her and made the call to Lilli's doctor. He got the answering service since it was a Saturday. "Lilli McCall is going to the hospital right now. I don't care who is on call. I expect to see Dr. Roberts at the hospital. My name is Max De Luca. I'm her husband."

He disconnected his cell and turned to find Lilli staring at him. "That's not how on call works. If you deliver on a weekend, you don't necessarily get your specific doctor."

"Not my wife," Max said.

She blinked and shook her head. "I'm not used to the idea of being your wife."

"I'll help you," he said in a dry tone. "Do you need to lie down?"

She shook her head and winced. "I'm too uncomfortable to lie down. The contractions are much stronger than they were with the false labor." Fear glinted in her eyes. She bit her lip and reached for his hand. "Max, I'm going to have a baby. I want him to be okay."

He pulled her into his arms. "He will be."

Within two hours of arriving at the hospital, Max could tell that Lilli was suffering. Her body tensed in pain. With each contraction, she stared straight ahead and did the breathing she'd learned in her prepared childbirth classes.

Her fingernails dug into his hands during the height of the pains. The sight of her dealing with such pain horrified him. He'd never known modern childbirth was so barbaric. A newfound respect for Lilli grew inside him.

"I think I want an epidural," she announced breathlessly after what looked like an excruciating contraction.

Relieved, he immediately called the nurse and demanded the medication.

After what felt like forever, the obstetrician checked Lilli's progress and shook her head. "Too late for an epidural."

Outraged, Max stood. "What do you mean too late? She's in pain. She needs medication and she'll damn well have it."

The doctor shot him a long-suffering look. "Mr. De Luca, the baby is crowning. Your wife is ready to deliver."

His wife. His son. The knowledge hit him like a ton of bricks. Within thirty minutes and what had to be a thousand pushes, the baby, a small squalling mass of humanity, made his entrance into the world.

The baby cried. Lilli cried. Max swore. Seconds later, Lilli held her son, *their son,* in her arms. "You're here," she said to the baby, touching each of his tiny fingers and toes. "You're really here." She looked up at Max, her eyes filled with tears. "Look. We did it."

Max shook his head. "You did all the work. I didn't do anything."

"Yes, you did," she said. "You were here for me. For him. You watched over me. I want you to hold him."

Max gingerly took the baby in his arms and looked down into the infant's face. "Nice hat," he said of the tiny blue cap the nurse had placed on his head. "He's—" Max paused. "He's pink."

Lilli laughed. "That's a good thing. It means he's healthy."

Max gave a slow nod and studied the baby. "Little hands. Soft skin. What are we going to call you? There's got to be something better than butter bean." He glanced at Lilli. "Do you know what you're going to name him?"

Lilli felt something inside her quiver and shake. Watching Max hold her son made her bones shift.

The baby waved a hand toward Max and he looked surprised. "Hi there," he said in a low voice. "Looks like your mom did an excellent job."

Lilli bit her lip as she felt another stabbing urge to cry.

Max returned the baby to her arms. "He looks perfect."

"Thank you," she said, blinking against threatening tears. "I think I want to name him David."

He nodded. "Excellent choice. Solid. Not trendy or ambiguous. He won't have to beat anyone up on the playground to defend his name."

She took a careful breath and watched his face. "And for his middle name, I was thinking of Maximillian."

He stared at her for a long moment in silence.

The longer the silence lasted the more nervous Lilli felt. Even the baby squirmed in her arms. "If it's okay with you," she added. "If you don't want that, then—"

"No, I do. I'm just surprised. I wondered if you would name him after Tony."

"You have already been more of a father to him than your brother could have ever been."

The next month passed in a blur of bottles, diapers and middle-of-the night interruptions. Lilli fell head over heels in love with her son, but when she showed the first sign of weariness, Max insisted she choose a mother's helper. Although she fought the idea at first, Lilli couldn't deny that getting a full night of rest made her feel like a new woman.

Since the baby had been born, Max continued to sleep in his room and she slept in hers. It seemed as though he was at work all the time. At first, she'd been too tired to focus on it, but now she was starting to get nervous. The more she thought about it, the more she realized he'd barely touched her during the last few weeks. Had his desire for her waned? Now that she was a mother, had she somehow become less sexy? The notion tortured her.

Unable to stand their polite distance any longer, she waited up for him one night. She sat in the dark, drinking her first glass of wine in ten months, rehearsing her conversation. She'd carefully chosen a silky camisole top and flowing blue skirt that made her feel feminine. She'd even put on a little makeup to perk up her features.

Sitting in the den, she turned on the lamp beside her and flipped through an architectural magazine. With only the soft glow from a lamp to keep her company, nine o'clock passed, then nine-thirty, then ten o'clock, but she was determined to wait for him.

It was close to ten-thirty when Max dragged himself through the door from the garage. He rubbed the back of his tense neck. These late hours were going to kill him.

But it wasn't as if he had any choice. He sure as hell couldn't hang around the house. Now that Lilli had delivered the baby, he had no visual reminder of why he couldn't take her to bed.

He would be an inconsiderate bastard to take her before she was fully recovered. That left him with the option of playing an exhausting game of keep-away. Sighing, he tugged his tie loose the rest of the way and unbuttoned the top few buttons on his shirt. Out of the corner of his eye, he noticed a light from the den. Curious, he walked into the room and found Lilli sleeping, her arms wrapped around a large throw pillow.

A stab of hunger twisted his gut. Lord help him, he was jealous of that damn pillow. He wanted her wrapped around him.

Her skirt had risen above her knees, revealing her shapely legs, and the material clung with sensual ease over her feminine curves. A strand of her hair had fallen over her cheek.

She was so inviting it was all he could do not to carry her up to his room right then. Instead, he tempted his self-control by lifting his fingers to touch that silky strand of hair and slide it away from her cheek.

Her lashes fluttered and she gradually opened her eyes. Her sexy, dazed expression lingered a few seconds before it cleared. "Hi," she said with a trace of self-consciousness and pushed herself up from the pillow. "I must have fallen asleep."

He nodded. "You're dressed up. Did you have plans?"

Her cheeks warmed with color and she pushed her hair from her face. "I was waiting up for you."

Surprise kicked through him and he sat down beside her. "Why? Is there a problem with David? Is the mother's helper still working out?"

"No problem with Maria. She's perfect. David is

perfect," she added and paused. "Although I would like you to spend a little more time with him."

He nodded. "I can do that. I just wanted to give the two of you time to get adjusted first."

She bit her lip and met his gaze. "Is that why you've also been avoiding me?"

"Caring for an infant is demanding, plus you need to recover from the birth."

She continued to look at him as if she were waiting for him to add something more. When he didn't, she sighed. "You're sure that's all there is?"

He frowned. "What else would there be?"

She bit her lip again. "I wasn't sure if perhaps you were having second thoughts about getting married. If, maybe…" She faltered then lifted her chin as if she were determined to go on. "If you didn't want me anymore."

Shock zinged through him like an electrical current. "You're joking, aren't you?"

"No, I'm not," she said, her voice husky. "You haven't touched me since the baby was born. You're always gone. What else should I think?"

"That I don't want to ravage you like some sex-starved bastard," he told her. "That I don't trust myself in the same room with you for more than five minutes."

Her eyes widened in surprise. "But you seem so detached."

"Lilli," he said, primitive need rising inside him, "I've been waiting to take you for a long time. I'm not sure how gentle I'll be."

Her gaze fixed on his, she licked her lips, sending another current of desire lashing through him. "So you really do still want me."

"Yes," he said in a voice he knew sounded rough around the edges.

Giving a sigh of relief, she moved closer to him and lifted her hand to his jaw. At her soft touch, he clenched his jaw. She rubbed her thumb over his mouth and he covered her hand with his. He slid that daring thumb of hers inside his mouth and gently bit the delicate pad.

He heard her soft intake of breath and put her hand away from him. "Don't push me."

She met his gaze for a long moment. "I go to the doctor on Friday."

"For what?"

"My follow-up visit. It's likely that I'll be released for all normal activity."

Wanting to remove any confusion on his part, he asked, "What does that include?"

"Everything," she said and lowered her voice to a whisper. "Including sex."

Max immediately felt himself grow hard with arousal. *Friday. Two days.* "I'd like you to give me a call after your visit," he told her.

"I know you told me not to push you," she said, moving closer to him again. "But can I kiss you?"

Max knew a cold shower was in his future tonight. "Come here," he said and pulled her across his lap.

She slid her fingers through his hair and gently pressed her mouth against his.

Desire raged through him. Her lips were petal soft, her body deliciously pliant. He wanted to touch her and take her every way a man could take a woman. When she dipped her tongue into his mouth, he thought he would explode.

A simple kiss, he thought, and he felt like a raving lunatic. Her breasts pressed against his chest and he wanted to tear off her dress, rip off his shirt and feel her nipples against his skin. He rubbed his hands over the side of her breasts and felt her shiver. With that small encouragement, he slid his fingers over her nipple and felt the stiff peak through her silky top.

Making a restless movement against him, she slid her tongue deeper into his mouth. His temperature rose and he began to sweat. She was so sweet, so tempting.

He knew he should stop, but he couldn't resist going a little further. He eased his hands under her top, surprised to find that she wore no bra. He wouldn't have thought he could get any hotter, especially knowing they couldn't finish tonight, but he did.

Taking control of the kiss, he slid one of his hands over her breast and swallowed her delicious gasp of arousal. "Do you want me to stop?" he asked against her mouth.

She shook her head. "It's been so—" She broke off and shuddered when he brushed her nipple with his thumb. "I never thought I could feel this way again."

"You couldn't have forgotten completely," he said in disbelief, nibbling at her bottom lip as he continued to caress her breast.

"I think I must have," she said and reached for the buttons to his shirt.

Not trusting himself any further, he covered her hand with his. "Later," he said. "Later."

Looking at her smoky eyes and lips puffy from their kisses, Max groaned. It took every ounce of fortitude not to take her mouth again.

She shook her head in disbelief. "After that last terrible time with Tony, I was sure I'd never want to be with a man again."

Max's arousal abruptly cooled. "You've mentioned this before. What was terrible about it?"

She glanced away. "I don't like to think about it. I don't like to talk about it. It's just that everything is so different with you."

"What happened with Tony?" he demanded.

She sighed. "He's your brother. There's no need to taint his memory any more than it already is."

"Lilli," he said. "I knew Tony had problems, most of which he made for himself. Heavy drinking, drugs, illegal deals. We weren't close. I'm your husband, now. You can't keep this kind of thing from me."

She twisted her fingers together. "I had already broken up with him once," she said in a low voice. "He promised things would be different, so I went out with him again. We went to a club and things were getting wild. I told him I wanted to leave. He begged me to stay for just one more dance, just one more drink. I just ordered soda."

Max got a dark feeling about what had happened with Lilli. "And?"

She bit her lip. "He put something in my drink. I woke up hours later and he had—"

Max felt a rush of nausea. He couldn't believe his own brother would do such a thing. "He took advantage of you without your consent?"

She closed her eyes and nodded. "I had told him I wasn't ready to be intimate again, that we had to take it slow. After that night, I broke things off permanently.

I realized I would never be able to trust a man who would do that to me."

Max's mouth filled with bitterness. He was so furious he wanted to break something. The strength of it caught him off guard.

Taking a mind-clearing breath, he reined in his anger and focused on Lilli. "I'm sorry he did that to you. I tried to steer Tony in the right direction, but he refused to listen." He slid his hand under her chin and guided her so she met his gaze. "I promise you I would never do something like that to you."

Her eyes were shiny with unshed tears. "You don't have to promise. I already know."

Max realized that Lilli would need to be seduced. It had been a long time for her and it would be his pleasure to remind her in every way that she was a desirable woman and that the passion between them would take her to a level she'd never experienced before. And as her husband, he would make damn sure no one ever hurt her again.

Eleven

Lilli envisioned that once she told Max the doctor had released her, the first thing Max would do was take her to bed. Instead he took her to dinner at the top of the premier Megalos-De Luca property in Vegas. With the baby in Maria's care, Lilli was free to enjoy herself.

Steeped in luxury, the resort featured an outdoor restaurant with a prized breathtaking view of the strip and beyond. "This is beautiful," she said for the umpteenth time after they enjoyed a delicious meal. "You really surprised me."

"I thought we both deserved a night out," he said, a cryptic grin crossing his face. "Think of this as the wedding dinner we skipped."

"For David," she said, laughing. Her heart skipped a beat at the sight of Max seated across the table from her. Dressed in a black suit, black shirt and tie, he looked dark and devastating. Tension and anticipation hummed between them. Every time Lilli thought about how the evening would end, her breath stopped in her throat.

She looked past the other empty tables at the night-time view of Las Vegas. "It's so sparkly," she said.

"So it is," he said and poured her another glass of Cristal.

"Why are there no other people here?"

"I ordered privacy," he said. "We can do anything we want," he added in a velvet, seductive voice.

Her heart hiccuped and she stared at the table. It was the first possibility that came to mind. "Omigoodness, you don't mean doing it here in public."

He laughed. "I said it's not public."

She sputtered. "B-but—"

Rising, he extended his hand. "Let's dance."

She distantly heard the strains of a romantic melody being piped through an outdoor sound system and im-mediately identified it. She stood and walked into his arms. "It's hokey, but this is one of my favorite songs."

He drew her close to him. "Old Elvis song sung by Michael Bublé. 'I can't help falling in love with you.'"

"How did you know?"

"I swiped your iPod."

"You are diabolical."

"I'll make you like it."

She had an unsettling feeling he could make her like a lot of things. She felt an achy tug in the region of her heart as she breathed in his scent and clung to his broad shoulders.

He nudged her head upward and took her mouth with his. He slid one of his hands behind her neck and she felt a sensual possessiveness in his touch. Her body immediately responded to his.

The sexy romantic song continued to play and she couldn't help feeling a little sad knowing that Max might want her, but would never really love her. The knowledge didn't keep a fire from building in her belly. The touch of his tongue and the way his body skimmed the front of hers made her blood pump with a primitive beat.

He pulled back slightly. Although his eyelids were hooded, she could still see a naked passion in them. "I've never waited this long for a woman," he said and dipped his open mouth to her neck. He drew her against him and she felt his unmistakable hardness. Sliding his hand over her bottom, he guided her against him.

"I want to taste every inch of you," he muttered against her mouth as he lifted one of his hands to her breast.

Lilli gave an involuntary shudder of anticipation.

"You like that," he said, more than asked. "I'm going to touch you all over." He slid his hand down over her hip.

The prospect took her breath away and she instinctively tried to get closer to him. She wanted to feel his skin. She wanted to slide her mouth over his chest and taste him. She wanted to see if she could make him sweat a little. Her blood pounding through her body, pooling between her thighs, she pulled his tie loose and tugged at the buttons to his shirt.

"I want to be closer, as close as I can get," she whispered breathlessly.

He swore and caught her hands against him. "This is our first time. I'll be damned if it's over in five minutes."

"You make me—" She broke off and swallowed over her dry throat. "Want."

His nostrils flared as he took several deep breaths. "Good. We'll finish this back at the house."

Burning with frustration, she allowed him to lead her from the restaurant. On the way down the elevator, she concentrated on trying to calm down. What must he think of her? That she was so easily aroused by him that she forgot about time and space?

He led her to the car and tucked her into the backseat, instructing Ricardo to take them to the house. He pressed the button for the privacy panel and turned to her. "Why so quiet?"

"I'm a little embarrassed," she quietly admitted, looking out the window.

"Why?"

She shrugged, not wanting to meet his gaze.

He slid his hand under her chin and made her look at him. "Why?"

"Because I would have had sex with you on one of the tables, and you were just—" She broke off and tried to look away, but he wouldn't allow it.

"Just what?"

"Just kidding or teasing," she said.

His dark eyes widened in disbelief. "You think I didn't want you back there?"

She bit her lip.

He swore. "Lilli, I've wanted you since the first time I saw you. I've been to hell and back a dozen times trying to keep my hands off you. You haven't had sex since you got pregnant. I don't want to rush things. I don't want to hurt you."

"Oh," she said, surprised he was so concerned about her discomfort. She'd known he had been determined to wait until the doctor released her, but this went further and oddly turned her on even more.

She impulsively slid her hands behind his neck and kissed him. She rubbed her breasts against his chest, straining to get as close as possible.

Max immediately slid his arms around her and kissed her back just as eagerly. The kiss seemed to go on and on and Lilli felt her temperature climb along with Max's.

He pulled his mouth just a breath away from hers. "I'm not complaining, but what was that for?"

"It was so sweet of you to be worried about hurting me," she whispered.

"That's your way of rewarding me for being sweet?" Max said. "Hell, no one has ever called me sweet before. Maybe I should be sweeter more often if this is how you react."

He took her mouth again and teased both of them into a frenzy by the time the chauffeur pulled into the driveway. Ricardo opened the door for them and Max helped her out of the car. After they climbed the steps to the porch and he opened the front door, he swung her into his arms and carried her inside.

"Wow," Lilli said, shocked again.

"For luck," he said. "I'm not usually superstitious, but I want to hedge my bets this time." Then he carried her upstairs to his master suite. When he set her down on the floor, he allowed her body to slide intimately down his, not hiding his arousal from her.

Lilli felt a quick shimmer of nerves and nearly suffocating anticipation. This was it. No turning back. "I bought a negligee, but it's in my room."

"Another time," he said and took her face in his hands and began to kiss her. His mouth was warm and sensual; the touch of his hands made her feel precious and sexy at the same time. Lilli felt the room begin to spin.

He unzipped her dress and pushed it down over her shoulders, waist and hips until it pooled at her feet. She pushed his jacket from his shoulders and fumbled with the buttons on his shirt. This time he didn't stop her.

Unsnapping her bra, he filled his hands with her breasts. Lilli let out a breath she hadn't known she'd been holding. Skimming his hands down her rib cage and waist, he cupped her bottom and rubbed her against his hard erection.

Taking her mouth in a French kiss, he looped a thumb beneath the waistband of her tiny silk panties and pushed them down. Lilli had thought she couldn't get any hotter, but she'd been wrong.

His fingers did maddening things to her, and she felt herself grow so swollen she could barely stand it. He made her ache. He made her acutely aware of the empty, needy sensation that she knew he could fill.

Tugging his belt loose, she unfastened and unzipped his slacks. Meeting his gaze, she pushed down his slacks and underwear.

"Touch me," he said.

She did. He was huge and hard in her hands and she couldn't help wondering if perhaps his concern about her discomfort may have been valid. She stroked him and he let out a hiss of breath. He closed his eyes while she caressed him.

"Not too much of that," he muttered and pulled her against him. Pushing away the rest of their clothes, he picked her up and carried her to his big bed. He reached over to his bed table and pulled a condom from the drawer.

Lilli took a shallow breath at the sight of him. His eyes were dark with need, his body was well-muscled, his erection huge. He reminded her of a prize stallion and some secret, primitive part of her was proud that she was the one he'd chosen.

He groaned and lowered his mouth to hers. Lilli thought he would take her at that very second. He was ready. She was ready. There was nothing stopping them. Finally.

Instead, he dipped his lips to her nipples and started making her crazy all over again. He slid one of his hands between her legs. She thought about protesting or begging. She didn't know which, but then she couldn't seem to breathe let alone say anything except the whisper that squeezed past her throat. "Please."

He drew the tip of her breast deep into his mouth and she arched toward him. "Please," she whispered again.

"What do you want, baby?" he asked her.

Shameless with need, dripping with want, she closed her eyes. "You. In me."

"Open your eyes," he said in a low, rough voice.

She did as he asked and he thrust inside her with one smooth, sure stroke.

She gasped. He moaned.

"Too much?"

She waited a few heartbeats for her body to adjust to his and shook her head. "More," she said.

Swearing under his breath, he pumped into her, driving his pelvis in a rhythm she echoed. The sensation of him filling her, stretching her, making her secret, wet places contract and shudder was almost overwhelming.

The feeling intensified with every stroke and Lilli lost control, splintering, spinning into orbit. Seconds later, she felt him stiffen and thrust one last time, groaning in release.

He lifted his head and pressed his mouth to hers, his kiss both tender and seductive. "Now, you're mine," he said.

Max kept her in bed for the next eight hours with very little sleep. At that point, he took a shower and returned some business calls. Lilli grabbed a quick shower, then took David from Maria, fed him, held him and bathed him.

Wide-awake, her baby watched her with big eyes and moved his mouth and made little sounds as if he were trying to talk with her.

"You've been such a good boy," Lilli told him. "Sleeping through the night. Maria was so happy and I am, too." She pulled a book from the basket beside the rocking chair and began to read. "'Once upon a time…'"

She alternated between reading and looking at his sweet face. The rapt attention in his big eyes made her smile. She tickled him under his chin and he wiggled. She did it again and he lifted the corners of his lips into a smile.

Joy and surprise rushed through her. "You smiled," she said and stood, bursting to share the news. "David smiled," she called down the hallway to anyone who would listen. "His first smile. David smiled for the first time."

Max rounded the corner, his cell phone pressed to his ear. "Just a minute, Jim. Something wrong?"

"No," Lilli said, rubbing her thumb under David's chin again. "David smiled for the first time."

Max looked at her first then at David, who was not smiling now. "Are you sure?"

"Yes, I'm sure. I just distracted him because I got so excited. I probably scared him," she said.

"Maybe it was gas."

"It was not gas," she said. "He doesn't smile when he has gas. He grimaces."

Max looked at her and David skeptically. "If you say so. I should wrap up this call with Jim. If David does it again, let me know."

He didn't believe her, she realized, and it bothered her. She wanted him to be as excited about David's firsts as she was. She wanted him to love David as much as— She broke off the thought. She was expecting way too much too soon, she told herself.

After a little more time, Max would grow to love David. He wouldn't be able to resist the child. It would be no time before David would be looking at Max with hero worship in his eyes. Surely a child's adoration would be able to penetrate the steel vault protecting Max's heart. Lilli just wasn't sure she could make it into his heart and maybe it was best if she didn't try.

* * *

Later that night after she fed David once more and put him to bed, she turned on the monitor and cracked the door to the nursery as she left the room. Bone tired, all she could think about was going to sleep. Max met her in the hallway holding two glasses of wine.

"Time for the rest of the honeymoon."

Despite her weariness, her pulse quickened at the seductiveness in his eyes. "If I drink a sip of that wine, I'll fall into a coma."

"Tired?" he asked, nudging the glass into her hand and guiding her down the stairs. "Baby wear you out with all his gas?"

She shot a dark look at him. "It wasn't gas. He was smiling."

"Did he do it again?" he asked.

"No, but—"

"Like I said."

"I'm the mother. I know," she said defiantly.

He lifted his lips in a half grin. "Can't argue with that," he said and clinked his glass against hers. He dipped his mouth over hers. "A meeting of the minds. Next, a meeting of the bodies. I think you might like a soak in the Jacuzzi."

It sounded wonderful. "I need my swimsuit."

He shook his head. "No, you don't."

Her heart jumped again. "Won't one of the staff see?"

"They're paid not to see."

"But still," she began.

"If your modesty is screaming that loudly," he said. "I can turn off the lights. Come on." He tugged her out the patio door and into the cool night air.

She shivered.

"The Jacuzzi will warm you up in no time."

It was easier being naked in front of him when they were in bed, when she didn't have time to think. She took a shallow breath. "You go first."

"Okay," he said and set their wineglasses beside the tub. He shucked his clothes without an ounce of self-consciousness. His tanned skin gleamed in the moonlight. His shoulders were broad, his belly flat, his buttocks firm.

Why should he be self-conscious? He had a body that should have been chiseled in marble. His face was hard, but when he smiled, he could turn her world upside down. And his eyes did things to her heart rate, her temperature, and her whole body.

He stepped into the Jacuzzi and turned to look at her. "Your turn."

She fought a rush of self-consciousness. "Turn off the light."

After he killed the light, she pulled off her shirt and jeans, then her bra and panties. Fortifying herself with another breath, she stepped into the tub. Despite the hot temperature, she plunged her body under the bubbles.

"Better?" he asked.

"Hot," she said, although she was grateful for the semicover of water.

His laugh rumbled all the way down between her legs. "You sound like Goldilocks. Too cold. Too hot. You even have the hair," he said, touching her hair before he slid his mouth over hers. His mouth was warm, his tongue seductive.

She felt some of the tension ease out of her.

"You have a beautiful body," he said against her lips. "I love the way your breasts respond to me." He lowered his hands to her nipples and plucked at them, turning them into hard orbs of sensation.

Making a sound of approval, he pulled her onto his lap. She balanced herself with her hands on his chest. His skin felt slick and sexy beneath her touch. Her thighs were slippery against his and the steamy water mirrored the heat between them.

He dipped his forehead against hers. "This wasn't such a bad idea, was it?"

Her breasts brushed against his chest, keeping her nipples taut and sensitive. "It's nice."

"I thought you would like it." Reaching behind him, he grabbed a remote and the strains of a saxophone eased around them. "Are you hungry? I can ask the housekeeper to bring something out—"

"I would drown so she wouldn't see me."

He chuckled and slid his arms around her. "I'll help you get over your shyness."

"Maybe with you," she said, her breath hitching when he fondled her breasts again.

"I wasn't sure how I would like being married, but so far I'm liking it," he said.

"So far is all of six weeks. But that reminds me of something," she said and tried to focus on something other than his muscular chest or how his hands felt on her or how his hard thighs felt under her bottom.

"What?"

"If we're going to make this marriage thing work—"

"We are," he interjected.

She nodded. "It occurred to me that I don't know what you want from me as your wife."

His eyes glinted with an irresistible sexy humor. "You've done very well so far."

"I didn't mean *that*. I mean when we're not in bed."

"We're not in bed right now," he reminded her, shifting her legs apart and pulling her intimately against him. He slid one of his hands between her thighs and moved his hand in a sensual, searching motion.

"I mean when we're not—" She broke off when he grazed the most sensitive part of her. "You're making it hard for me to concentrate."

"That's because you're concentrating on the wrong thing," he said. "I want you to concentrate on what you're feeling right now." He sank deeper into the water and slipped his hand under her bottom, pushing her upward so that her breasts bobbed directly in front of his face.

He lowered his head and took one of her nipples into his mouth. The sight of his dark head against her pale skin sent a hot current to the most sensitive pleasure points in her body. His thumb found her again and a delicious haze fell over her.

It didn't matter that things between them felt so unsettled. It didn't matter that they were outside and if someone really wanted to watch them, they could. What mattered was that she was in his arms and the water made her feel both relaxed and eager. He was looking at her as if she was his first meal in a long time, and she knew firsthand that it hadn't been very long at all.

She slid her hand down between them and found him already hard. He gave a sensual groan and leaned backward on one of the graduated steps, looking at her through hooded eyes. "How am I supposed to go slow if you're going to touch me like that?"

"You want me to stop?"

"Oh, no," he said and pulled her over him and took her mouth in a kiss that made her feel consumed and restless. "You have no idea how sexy you look," he muttered and cupped her bottom, guiding her over him. His pelvis flexed upward and she sank down onto him. With her hair spilling forward, she kissed him. His tongue filled her mouth with the same rhythm he filled her lower body. Slow and easy, the erotic motion made her dizzy with pleasure.

He squeezed her bottom. She lifted her mouth for a breath and he drew one of her nipples deep into his mouth. "You make me so greedy," he said.

He made her desperate to please him. At the same time, though, he made sure she was pleasured. She'd thought she would be too sore, too sensitive, but the water cushioned their movements.

Steam rose around them. Tiny droplets dotted his face. His dark eyes were glazed with arousal. He continued to rub and she matched his pace, her nether regions tightening with every stroke. She felt the peak start in her breasts and shower down to where she convulsed around him, her muscles contracting around his hardness.

His eyes narrowed as he gasped in pleasure, surging into her. "Oh, Lilli."

When he said her name, an aftershock coursed through her, and she realized what she craved. She wanted this to be more than good sex for Max. She wanted it to mean something to him. *She* wanted to mean something to him. Fear prickled inside her. It wouldn't be a good idea to want these kinds of things from a man who didn't believe in romantic love. She needed to figure out how to stay safe and sane.

He took her mouth in a kiss and moved sideways in the bubbling water, still inside her, her legs laced with his muscular thighs. Sanity was the last thing she could muster.

Twelve

The following morning, Max rose early. He felt an itchy sensation in his back. He felt crowded, yet at the same time, he would have liked to stay in bed and enjoy his wife's charms. Instead, he took a shower and was putting on his tie just as Lilli awakened.

She rubbed the sleep from her eyes and glanced at the alarm clock. "It's only six o'clock. You're going into the office already?"

"There's a lot waiting for me. I'll be home late tonight."

"What's late?"

He shrugged. "Maybe nine."

She nodded slowly. "Can I get you some breakfast?"

He shook his head as he straightened his tie. "I'm going straight to the office. My assistant will bring something."

Pulling the sheets up to her shoulders, she met his gaze in the mirror. Her hair was sexily rumpled and she blinked her eyes as she obviously tried to make herself wake up. The skin around her chin was pink from the effects of his beard.

He would need to be more careful in the future, he thought as he rubbed his just-shaven jaw. Her skin was sensitive and he'd mauled her from head to toe during the last two days. The vulnerability in her eyes made him want to hold her, but something else made him want to run.

He walked toward her. "Have a good day, lovely Lilli," he said in a light voice and, not trusting himself, he dropped an even lighter kiss on her cheek.

"You, too," she said. "If David smiles, I'll try to catch it with my camera phone. I'll send you a message."

The offer made his chest feel tight. "You mean if he has gas?" he teased and opened the bedroom door to leave. But not before he felt a pillow hit him in the back of the head. He whipped around, staring at her in surprise. Her hand covered her mouth as if she'd surprised herself, too. It didn't help his concentration that she'd dropped the sheets and her breasts were bared to his sight.

Steeling himself against the distraction and the hard-on growing harder by the moment, he looked down at her and shook his head. "You had me fooled. I thought you were an angel except when I got you in bed."

She bit her lip, but couldn't seem to prevent the beginning of a saucy smile. "I'm still in bed."

"So you are," he said and wished like hell he were there with her. "See you tonight."

* * *

Maybe it shouldn't have felt abrupt for Max to leave so early, but it did. Lilli pulled the sheet over her head and told herself to go back to sleep. She tried to push aside her feelings, but she felt bothered, unsettled. Was this the future for their marriage? Strangers everywhere except when they shared a bed?

Groaning, she threw off the sheet and climbed out of bed. Sore and tired, she wished she could grab a few extra winks, but she knew her mind wasn't going to let her. Grumbling to herself, she took a shower. Her body was sensitive, and she ached in secret places. She allowed the hot water to flow over her, willing it to soothe the tenderness in her muscles. And her heart.

After she dressed, she gave Maria a well-deserved break and listened for David's cry. He'd barely let out a sound before she gathered him to her and fed him. As he devoured his bottle, she noticed tiny beads of perspiration break out on his forehead.

"You are very intense about your food, aren't you, sweetie?" she said.

Moments later, he finished and she squeezed a couple burps out of him. She looked down into his face and smiled at him. He smiled back. Delighted, Lilli drank in his joyful expression. Then she remembered she needed to take a photograph, so Max would believe her. Jumping up from the rocking chair, she ran to grab her cell phone and positioned it over David's face, ready to take a photo. David, however, was less interested in smiling and more fascinated with the object in her hand. The smile had disappeared.

"Well, darn," she muttered. She smiled again and he looked at her with solemn eyes as he blew bubbles. "That's just as cute as a smile," she said and took the photo and sent it to Max anyway.

She took David for a stroll around the block. Just as she was turning into the driveway, her cell phone rang. Her heart racing, she didn't bother to check the caller ID because she was sure it was Max. "Hi there," she said.

"Hi, Lilli," an unfamiliar voice said. "This is Devon."

Lilli stopped midstep and swallowed a sudden foolish twinge of disappointment. Devon, one of the hospice attendants to her mother, he had been with them until the very end. "Oh, Devon, I haven't heard from you in a while. How are you? How are your parents?"

"Dad's not doing so well. He's in the final stages of cancer and my mother was just admitted to the hospital. They want to put her on dialysis."

Sympathy surged through her. "I'm so sorry. Is there anything I can do?"

"I didn't want to ask, but you told me to call you if things got out of control. I'm staying with my father around the clock, so I'm not making any money."

"I understand," she said. "How much do you need?"

"It depends," Devon said, his voice choking up. "On how soon my father goes. Oh, God, I can't believe I said that."

"No, I understand. I took off a lot of time to be with my mother at the end."

"I don't want him to die, but—" He broke off again and sighed. "You would think that since I work in a hospice, I would be better prepared for this."

"It's much more personal," Lilli said. "It's your father. Listen, why don't I bring you some money to tide you over? I've forgotten your address. Give it to me again."

Devon gave her the address. "I'll probably need to call you back for directions. Would you like me to sit with your father so you can get out for a while?"

"I couldn't do that to you," he said. "I feel bad enough asking for financial help."

"You forget how great you were with my mother when she was so sick. You were there for us. I'd like to be there for you."

"But that was my job."

"Well, you did an amazing job and my mother and I couldn't thank you enough. So let this be a little token. I'll come over this afternoon around three. David should be napping."

"Ah, the baby. How is he?" Devon asked.

"Perfect," she said.

He laughed. "As if he could be anything else since he came from you."

She smiled. "Please keep your cell handy, in case I get lost."

"Will do, Lilli, and thanks," Devon said.

Lilli drove her little Toyota instead of the monster SUV Max had bought for her use. She left David in Maria's caring arms. After stopping by the grocery store to pick up a few things for Devon and his family, she only got lost twice, but finally arrived at Devon's apartment complex.

Devon greeted her at the door, but his father had taken a turn for the worse, so he refused to accept Lilli's offer to sit with his father so that Devon could get out for a little while.

Lilli gave the dark gentle giant a hug and left. The visit brought back memories of her mother's time in hospice. Lilli had been forced to hide the gnawing grief she'd felt in anticipation of her mother's death. Losing her mother inch by inch had been excruciating, but she wouldn't trade a moment of the time she'd had with her.

The familiar feeling of being all alone hit her as she stopped at a traffic light. She'd never known her father. Her mother was gone. Even though she was married, she sometimes still felt alone. Her chest grew heavy, her throat tightened and her eyes began to burn. Tears streamed down her face and she tried to comfort herself.

She had David. She had her little baby. She wasn't alone. The thought soothed her and she made a turn when the light turned green. Twenty minutes later, she realized she was horribly lost.

She reluctantly called Devon, but he wasn't picking up. She thought about stopping at a convenience store, but several men sat outside on the ground drinking from bottles in brown bags.

Lilli began to fuss at herself. "Should have done MapQuest. It would have taken three minutes. Three minutes." She rounded the corner and, spotting a small grocery store, she pulled into the tiny parking lot and went inside. The owner spoke very little English, but gave her directions to the interstate.

She followed the directions, or so she thought, but just found herself deeper into another area where she'd never been. At six-thirty, she gave up the fight and called Max's driver, Ricardo. He offered to come and get her, but she refused, embarrassed by her lack of a sense of direction.

Ricardo gave her turn by turn directions. Once she arrived at the interstate, she sagged with relief. Ricardo didn't want to hang up, but Lilli insisted she would be fine. She pulled into the garage an hour later and was surprised to see Max's car.

She smiled as she bounded up the stairs from the garage. Walking through the corridor, she looked for him in the foyer. She spared a quick glance into the den and noticed the patio door was open. Still dressed in his business attire, he stood outside with a bottle of water in his hand.

Lilli rushed to the patio. "Hi. You're home early," she said, unable to disguise her delight.

He turned to look at her. "And you're home late," he said in a voice that could cut glass. His eyes were cold. "Where have you been?"

Lilli winced when she remembered the discussion she'd had with Max about visiting suspicious areas of town. "I visited a friend and got a little lost driving back."

"Ricardo told me you called him from one of the worst neighborhoods in the city," Max said.

She could feel anger emanating from him. "Like I said, I got all turned around. I should have used MapQuest."

"If this was such a good *friend*," Max said. "Why would you need directions to their house?"

Lilli refused to squirm. She'd done nothing wrong. "I haven't been there very often. But I'm back now," she said cheerfully. "I need to check on David."

"Maria has him," he said. "Who was the friend?"

Lilli bit her lip. Darn, she'd hoped to avoid a confrontation. "It was Devon. His father has taken a turn for the worse, but he's lingering and Devon's mother is in the hospital."

"You didn't give him money, did you?"

"Yes, I did," she said without batting an eye. "I took him some groceries, too. I would have sat with Devon's father so he could get some fresh air, but his father was very ill this afternoon. Devon didn't want to leave him."

"You shouldn't let this guy take advantage of you."

"He didn't," Lilli said. "I was happy to write him a check." She paused a second and pressed her lips together. "I didn't take the money out of your account. I took it out of a savings account I set up with the small amount my mother left me."

"That's not the point. The point is that this man could be taking advantage of you," Max said.

"He's not. He has a heart of gold," she said, then corrected herself. "Maybe gold isn't the best description. He has a soft, sweet heart. No hard metals included."

"Unlike your husband with the steel heart," he said.

"I didn't say that," she said. "I just don't think you comprehend that Devon is a good soul."

"Who lives in a terrible area of town."

"Not everyone can afford to live up on the hill like you."

"We discussed this. You weren't going to visit him again without telling me."

"I never really agreed," she said. "But I'm an adult. I don't think I should be hassled because I want to help someone who was so good to my mother when she was dying."

"You can't put yourself in danger like that. You have a son to think about. You have people counting on you."

People? As in plural? Her heart stammered. She studied his face and moved toward him. "What are you really upset about?"

He met her gaze for a moment that seemed to last forever then let out a long breath. "I don't want anything to happen to you."

"It didn't."

"But it could have. Next time you feel the urge to go into a questionable neighborhood, will you please at least take Ricardo with you?"

"What if he's busy?"

"Then either wait until he isn't, or call me."

The worry in his voice took some of the air out of her defiance. "Okay," she said. "But if you start fussing at me, I'll stop listening."

He nodded and they stood silently watching each other. Wary. Lilli felt as if she were being pushed and tugged at the same time, as much from herself as from Max. The sound of David's cry broke the tension.

"I'd better check on him," she said.

"Have you had dinner?"

She shook her head.

"Neither have I. We can eat out here."

"Okay. I'll be back down in a little bit," she said and went upstairs to the nursery. Lilli did the bottle, bath and bed routine for David, but the baby was still wide-awake when she put him to bed. She read him some stories and rocked him, but he still didn't fall asleep.

Giving up, she took him downstairs with her and put him in a springy infant seat in a chair beside hers. Her stomach growled at the sight of the food in front of her. Max set down the newspaper he'd been reading. "Is someone not sleepy?"

"I think he wants to play soccer or basketball and he's very frustrated that he can't yet."

Max's lips twitched.

She turned on the Jacuzzi.

Max looked at her in alarm. "You're not really going to put him in the hot tub?"

"No, I was thinking the sound of the bubbles might soothe him."

"Good idea," he said.

"And if that doesn't work, maybe he would like to hear a male voice."

Max lifted his eyebrows. "Mine?"

She took a bite of her dinner. "You could read to him."

"What?" he asked, pointing at the paper beside him. "The *Wall Street Journal?*"

"Sure. That should put him right to sleep, don't you think?"

"If you say so," he said and began to read an article about the economy.

David kicked and wiggled. He made a neutral sound that Lilli suspected could turn into a fussy sound. "It would work better if you hold him."

Max looked at her. Her hair was fairy flyaway as usual and she had a crumb on the corner of her mouth. She gave him a huge, encouraging smile and damn if he didn't feel tempted to do anything for her. Including holding a potentially fussy baby.

"Okay, I'm game. Any tips?"

She set her fork down and jumped up from her chair.

"He likes to be held close," she said, picking David up from the infant seat and placing him in Max's arms. "He feels more secure when his arms and legs aren't flopping all over the place."

It presented a new challenge to hold the newspaper at the same time as he held David, but he was up for it. He'd conducted billion-dollar deals, and he'd been player of the year for his college soccer team. He had the right stuff for this. Max continued to read, but David still squirmed.

"Sometimes it helps if you jiggle him," Lilli said and took another bite from her plate, seemingly content to watch him struggle.

Max jiggled the baby and struggled to read the article from the newspaper that also jiggled from his movements. He made up a few of the words that got blurry. Actually, he began to make up entire sentences. "And then the economy got kicked on its ass due to the price of oil."

"I do not believe that statement was in the *Wall Street Journal*," Lilli said.

Max glanced down at David, whose eyes were closed. The baby slept peacefully in his arms. He felt as if he'd just made a goal in soccer or landed a huge deal. "It doesn't matter," he said in a low voice, "because I have successfully put our son to sleep."

He glanced up and looked at Lilli. She stared at him, her eyes shiny. "Yes, you did," she whispered. "But can you put him into his crib without waking him up?"

Another challenge. His competitive spirit piqued, he ditched the paper and carefully rose to his feet. "And what do I get if I succeed?"

"A pat on the back?" she said, covering her mouth as she muffled a chuckle.

"Lower," he said. "And not on the back."

Her blue eyes lit and smoldered. "Okay. If you can lay him down in the crib and he stays asleep, you can have whatever you want. I'll warn you, though, that he usually wakes up and needs to be rocked or walked a little longer."

"We'll see," he said, more motivated than ever.

Lilli stood. "And you need to put him to sleep on his back or on his side placed against the crib rail."

"Okay," he said.

"And make sure the blanket doesn't cover his face."

"Got it."

"And kiss him good-night."

"Kiss him?"

She nodded. "It's a requirement for a good night of sleep."

"I'll remember that," he said.

He could see her cheeks bloom with color even in the moonlight. "I'll be back in a few minutes."

"If you have to pick him up again, then it doesn't count."

"For what?" he asked. "You won't go to bed with me?"

She bit her lip. "I didn't say that."

"Give me a couple minutes. I'm an amateur at this, remember?"

Her gaze softened. "Yeah, I'll be waiting upstairs."

"Don't you want to finish your dinner?"

"That won't take two minutes," she said.

He smiled and she immediately smiled in response. Then he turned and took the baby up to the nursery, coaching himself and David. "You want to stay asleep," he said to David. "You're tired. You're ready to sleep until morning. You're worn-out. You've got a full belly and you're ready for your nice bed. You'll dream of warm bottles and walks in the stroller and being held in Lilli's arms. Can't argue with that last one, big guy."

He carefully walked toward the crib and continued to hold David, studying the baby's face. The baby looked as if he were totally out. Leaning over, millimeter by millimeter, he extended his arms and David stirred. Max immediately stopped, suspended over the crib.

David quieted and pursed his lips. Max counted to twenty then moved a few more inches. David wiggled slightly and Max stopped again. Patience was clearly the name of this game. He counted to twenty and moved several more inches. This time, David didn't stir. He extended the last few inches and carefully laid him sideways on the crib, leaving the blanket wrapped around him.

David wiggled and wiggled, but Max kept his hand on the baby and surprise, surprise, his son settled down.

Then he remembered the kiss. Max swallowed an oath. Surely it couldn't be that important. The baby was asleep. That was what was important, right?

Bowing to a combination of his Type A personality and his conscience, because he knew Lilli would ask about the kiss, he carefully lowered the side of the bed. He bent over and pressed a silent kiss on David's head then rose and slowly, slowly lifted the side of the crib. It made a loud clicking noise when it locked into place, making Max grimace.

He closed his eyes, waiting for David to make a

sound. A moment passed and all was still quiet. Max opened one eye, looked down at his son and was thrilled to see that the baby was asleep.

He took a deep breath and sighed. Now to collect his reward. He left the nursery and left a sliver of a crack between the door and the jamb. Walking into his bedroom, he stepped inside and found Lilli sitting in the middle of his bed wearing a white lace teddy that managed to look both innocent and naughty. Her rosy nipples showed through the transparent lace, as did the shadow between her thighs. His fingers itched to pull the skimpy garment from her, to bare her body to his gaze. He curled his hands into a fist then forced himself to release them.

"Very nice," he said. "How did you know I would succeed in getting David to stay asleep?"

"Aside from the fact that you're an overachiever?" she asked.

He couldn't keep his lips from twitching. "Yes."

"I wanted to thank you for the effort."

He tugged his shirt over his head then shucked his jeans and underwear so he stood before her completely naked. He saw her gaze gravitate to his erection and felt himself grow even harder. "How do you want to thank me?" he asked.

"Come here," she said and opened her arms. The gesture was so artless and open that it took his breath. He slid over the bed, pulling her against him, enjoying every millimeter of her silky skin against his.

"You feel so good," she whispered.

"I was going to say the same about you," he said, and dipped his head to kiss his way down her throat. When he reached her collarbone, he gently nibbled. Her sigh made him feel as if he were ready to burst.

"You're going to make this hard for me, aren't you?" he muttered, lowering his mouth to her breast, pushing the delicate fabric aside. He slipped his hand between her thighs and found her already wet and swollen. She squirmed beneath him and he felt his heart hammer against his rib cage.

She slid one of her hands between them and captured his bare erection in her hand. "I think you already started out—" She paused and shoved him onto his back. "Hard," she said and flowed down his body like silk.

The sensation of her open mouth on his chest, followed by his belly, took his breath. She waited three breaths and the anticipation nearly made him insane. Then she moved lower and took him into her mouth. The sight of her with her fairy angel hair, good girl/bad girl teddy, and her lips wrapped around him was one of his sexiest fantasies come true.

He watched her until he couldn't stand it any longer, then rolled her over, unsnapped her teddy and plunged inside her. He couldn't get enough of her—her passion, her sweetness. It was crazy, but being with her made him believe in possibilities he hadn't considered before.

After Max took her over the top twice and finally gave in to his own release, he held her against him for several moments. Neither of them said a word, but the power and pleasure of their lovemaking vibrated between them. He gently turned her over and pulled her back against him, stroking her hair.

His touch mesmerized her and she relaxed to the point that she almost fell asleep. She felt safer and more cherished than she'd felt in her entire life.

"I missed you today," he whispered into her ear.

Her heart stopped. His admission was the closest he'd come to professing any emotion. In her heart, she hoped it was just a step away from *I love you*. It took everything inside her not to make her own confession because she knew it would only burden him. He wasn't ready to hear that sometime along the way, she'd fallen in love with him.

Max woke to the sensation of Lilli's hands on his face. "Hey, Mr. Sunshine, the alarm is on your side of the bed."

Max blinked, opening his eyes to the sight of Lilli, with sleepy eyes, sexy puffy lips and the sound of one of Beethoven's symphonies from his alarm clock. He shook his head to clear it. He must have slept so soundly that he didn't hear his alarm when it first went off. He reached over and turned it off.

He never hit the snooze button and he always got out of bed within ten seconds. Glancing over at Lilli, he paused a good sixty.

"If you're going to stare at me, you can at least make yourself useful and hug me, too."

He chuckled and rolled back toward her, pulling her against him. She snuggled her breasts to his chest and pressed a kiss to his neck. Her body felt like silk.

Growing hard, he groaned. "The problem with holding you when you're naked is that I want to do a lot more than hold you."

"What's stopping you?" she asked in a sexy sleep-husky voice.

She might as well have lit a match next to a gas pump. He took her with a thoroughness that left both of them gasping for air.

Reluctantly, he dragged himself from bed. He looked back at her, nude, with a dazed, just-taken expression on her flushed face. He couldn't resist going back for one more kiss from her petal-soft lips, then forced himself to pull away.

Just as he reached the door to the bathroom, he heard her voice. "You can call me during the day if you want. It's not required," she quickly added. "But you can if you want."

She heard him last night after all, he realized. His heart gave a strange stutter. He couldn't tell if it was pleasure or pain. He'd gone skydiving a few times, and this sensation reminded him of free-falling out of an airplane. Was this what it felt like to fall for a woman? He swore under his breath. He didn't have the time to think about it right now.

"Thanks for the invitation," he said and headed for the shower.

Over the next few days after Lilli moved into Max's bedroom, Lilli felt almost like a newlywed. Max arrived home early. They shared dinner and took care of David then retired to Max's bed for nights of amazing lovemaking. She began to hope that he would eventually love her.

Saturday night after they'd visited a park and enjoyed a gourmet picnic prepared by Max's chef, they returned home. David had been fussy most of the afternoon. She fed him part of an extra bottle, hoping he would settle down, but he continued to fuss. She noticed he felt warm to the touch and took his temperature. It was elevated, but not overly so. Still, every time she tried to put him in his crib, his little body stiffened and he cried until he shook.

Max stepped inside. "Does he need another dose of the *Wall Street Journal?*"

She shook her head. "I don't think he's feeling well."

His demeanor immediately changed. "Does he have a temperature?"

"Not much of one," she said, showing him the thermometer. "All the baby books say to keep calm. But I think I may need to take him to the doctor tomorrow."

Max nodded in agreement.

"It may be a long night," she told him. "He's only calm when I hold him."

"I can understand that," he said, meeting her gaze, making her stomach jump at his double meaning. "I'll take a turn holding him if you can't get him settled."

"Thanks," she said and sighed when he gave her and David a hug. His arms felt so solid, so strong.

"Wake me to take a turn," he told her again.

"Maybe later," she said, but she didn't ask him. She finally succeeded in getting David settled and crawled into bed. She kept the nursery monitor directly beside her and heard him when he awakened in the middle of the night with a heart-tugging wail.

Max stirred beside her. "What is—"

"No, I'll take care of it," she said, quickly climbing out of bed and heading for the nursery. She almost collided with Maria, who'd already picked David up.

"Oh, the little sweetheart, he's burning up with fever," Maria said. She made a tsking sound. "He got sick in his bed."

"Oh, no. Let me hold him," Lilli said, taking him into her arms and biting her lip at the heat emanating from his tiny body. She pressed the thermometer against his ear, aghast at how quickly it had risen.

Fear clutched at her. David began to cry. "I wish I knew what was wrong with you, sweetie. I wish you could tell me where you hurt." David gave a high-pitched scream and Lilli fought a rising tide of panic.

Max stepped inside the room. "What's wrong?"

"His fever has gone up and he got sick in his bed," Lilli said, holding him close to her as she stroked his forehead.

As David let out another scream, Max nodded his head decisively. "Okay, that's it. We're taking him to the emergency room."

Thirteen

There was no wait at the emergency room for David Maximillian De Luca. It seemed everyone knew that Max had made generous donations to the Children's Hospital. The admissions tech quickly took down the insurance information and escorted Max, Lilli and David behind a curtain.

Max looked at David, who was clearly in pain, and felt his gut wrench. His son. It was his responsibility to alleviate his pain.

A very young woman in a white coat stepped inside the curtained cubicle. She picked up the chart and glanced at it. "Are you the parents?" she asked.

"Yes, we are."

"I'm Dr. Jarrett." She extended her hand and shook his. "Let's see what's wrong with your son."

Lilli continued to hold David close, cradling his head as he let out cries and sobs. As Dr. Jarrett looked inside David's right ear, the baby howled and the doctor winced. "I think I've found the problem. An ear infection. A nasty one at that." She rubbed the baby's head. "We can take care of that, sweetheart.

"We'll start him on antibiotics right away, and I have some other recommendations for pain. The good news is that these little guys tend to respond to antibiotics within twenty-four hours or less."

"Thank goodness," Lilli said. "He's been miserable."

"And he made sure you knew it, too, didn't he?" the doctor said with a smile.

"Yes, I guess he did." Lilli met Max's gaze. "I'm glad we came."

"Me, too," he said and asked the doctor a few more questions. Dr. Jarrett left David's file open on the tray while she left the area for a moment. Max glanced at the file, seeing David's birth information, his height, weight and blood type. He digested the information without focusing on it. The doctor returned, apologizing for the interruption.

After picking up the medication from the hospital pharmacy, Max helped Lilli administer it to David. He ushered both of them to his car, and David fell asleep on the way home.

Max pulled into the driveway and Lilli put her hand on his elbow. "I'm afraid to take him out of the infant seat," she confessed.

Max chuckled. "We can't leave him in the car the rest of the night."

"It's almost morning," she said and reached closer

to touch his jaw. "You are so amazing. And I am so lucky."

His heart swelled in his chest. "Why do you say that?"

"Because I was ready to panic over what to do about David, and you knew what to do immediately."

"You would have figured it out."

"Thank you," she whispered and kissed him. "I know you don't believe in love, but you're making me fall in love with you."

He didn't say anything, but she made him feel ten feet tall. She made him feel as if he could conquer anything and he wanted to do it for her and David.

He took a breath to clear his head. "We need to put him to bed," he said.

"Yeah," she said reluctantly.

"We can do it," he encouraged her. "We can do it together."

She nodded as if she found strength in his words. "Sure we can. Okay, let's go."

Surprisingly enough, David only gave a few peeps between the car seat and the crib. He made just enough sound to reassure Max and Lilli that he was uncomfortable, but okay. Lilli placed him in the crib and appeared to hold her breath.

David continued sleeping and Lilli let out a sigh.

"Time for Mama to get some sleep," Max said, taking her hand and leading her to bed.

She insisted on brushing her teeth then fell asleep as soon as her head hit the pillow. Max wasn't so lucky. Something nagged at him. He couldn't quite put his finger on it, but something he'd seen or observed at the hospital still bothered him.

Propping his hand behind his head on his pillow, he mentally backtracked his way through the evening.

Finally he remembered viewing David's file, his birth record, his weight. His blood type. His brother's blood type didn't match David's. Lilli's blood type had been listed above David's. David's didn't match hers, either.

He shook his head in disbelief. There had to be something wrong, a mix-up. But insidious doubts poked at him. If not Tony, then who was David's biological father?

The next question hit him so hard his chest squeezed tight with the pain. If not Tony, then who had been Lilli's lover?

Max felt nausea back up into his throat. Realization coursed through him like a slow-moving poison. Sitting up, he felt himself break into a sweat. Had she deceived him? Had sweet, angelic Lilli who'd baked cupcakes for his birthday pulled off the ultimate charade?

She'd made him believe she was going to give birth to his brother's son. With her wide blue eyes and fairy hair, she'd looked so innocent, so pure. And she'd played him to the hilt when she hadn't accepted his repeated offers for money.

He looked over at her sleeping in his bed as his wife and nearly drowned in disgust for himself. Shaking his head, he rose from the bed and thought of the way his father had acted like a fool over a woman. Max had made a vow to himself never to lose his head over a woman. But he'd gone and done just that.

Caught in semisleep, Lilli struggled to open her eyes. They felt as if someone had placed sandbags on top of them. She forced them to open. It took several minutes for her to become conscious.

Her first thought was of David. Her second was of Max. She looked beside her on the bed to find her husband gone. Type-A overachiever, she thought then glanced at the clock—8:00 a.m. She immediately pushed aside the covers and headed for the nursery. No one had called her, she reminded herself, as she stepped inside to find David being fed by Maria.

The nanny smiled. "He's much better this morning. Just a little cranky. A few more doses of his medication and he will be good as new."

David was focused on his bottle, clearly intent on getting every last drop. Lilli gave a sigh of relief. "Thank you for getting up with him."

"My pleasure," Maria said. "Mister De Luca is downstairs. He asked for you to go see him after you wake up."

"He's not at work?" Lilli asked, surprised.

Maria shook her head. "No. He's downstairs."

"Thank you again," Lilli said and returned to the bedroom to throw on some clothes, wash her face and put on some concealer. She didn't want to make a practice of looking like a hag first thing in the morning.

She went downstairs and spotted him on the patio. He sat on one of the plush chairs, staring at the fountain next to the Jacuzzi. Admiring his strong profile, she felt a rush of love. She gave herself a mental pinch. *This was her husband.*

She walked toward him and smiled. "Good morning, Mr. Amazing." She shook her head. "I don't see how you can go to sleep after I do, and still get up earlier than I do."

He met her gaze, but his eyes were cold. "I have things on my mind." He set his coffee cup on the patio table. "I saw David's medical file at the hospital last night."

"Is he okay? Is there something wrong that they didn't tell us?"

He lifted his hand. "No, no. Not that. What I noticed was David's blood type. It didn't match yours."

Max watched her carefully.

"Then it must match Tony's," she said, as if she were certain.

Feeling his gut begin to twist and turn, he shook his head. "No, it doesn't."

Lilli frowned. "It has to. There must be some mistake."

Max sat silently for a long moment. Awed by her ability to lie without so much as a twitch, he continued to study her. "There's no mistake, Lilli. David's blood type doesn't match Tony's. Tony cannot be David's biological father."

She stared at him for a long moment. "He is," she said her voice rising. "There's no other possibility. There's no—"

"Are you sure?" Max asked. "Who else did you have sex with while you were seeing my brother?"

Her mouth dropped wide in horror. "No one, I mean—" She broke off. "I wouldn't—"

She was still sticking to her story, but he was beginning to see some cracks in her composure. "Funny, that's what I thought, too."

"No, really," she said, knitting her fingers together. "I didn't have sex with anyone else. Tony has to be David's biological father. There's no other possibility," she said. "There was no one else. How could it be anyone else?"

Max stared at her in silence. Disappointment stabbed at him. Some part of him had held out hope that she would be honest with him. That she would give him that much.

Panic shot across her face and she ran to him. "You must believe me. You must. That blood test is wrong. It has to be. It has to—"

He stepped aside before she could touch him. He didn't want her to touch him. He didn't want his body to betray him. There was only one explanation for her hysteria. She had indeed lied to him and she was terrified of losing her meal ticket.

"I need to leave," he said and headed for the door.

"Max," she called after him, her voice full of tears and desperation.

But Max kept on walking.

Watching him leave, Lilli felt her throat and chest close so tight she could hardly breathe. He didn't believe her. He thought she had deceived him. Her heart died a little with each step he took away from her.

She sank into her chair, feeling as if she were going to splinter into a million pieces. How had this happened? *What* had happened? *Who* had done this to her?

Her mind reeled and she tried in vain to remember more details of that last fateful night with Tony. It had been hard enough for her to deal with the idea of Tony taking advantage of her, but knowing some anonymous faceless monster had done this to her made her feel more victimized than ever.

How could Max believe her when she couldn't believe it herself? And now he hated her. She'd read it on his face as clear as the writing on their prenup, on their marriage certificate and on the adoption papers.

She closed her eyes and felt her stomach and chest twist so hard she feared she would get sick. She broke into a cold sweat. Her mind raced. If he hated her, then how much more would he hate David?

Her first instinct was to leave. To get as far away from Max and this house as she could.

But why? She had done nothing to be ashamed of. She was the victim.

But she wouldn't be the victim any longer.

All day at work, Max tried to wrap his mind around the idea that Lilli had deliberately deceived him. But as his anger had cooled, he had trouble believing it. If she was acting, she could win an Academy Award.

She'd been stunned when he'd confronted her, certain there'd been a mistake. Her face had been full of confusion, horror and disbelief. Everything he'd been feeling.

If she'd truly been after his money, wouldn't she have insisted on more in the prenup agreement? He sat in his office, gazing blindly at the mountains in the distance. None of this added up. She had looked at him in complete disbelief when he told her Tony couldn't be David's father.

Pinching the bridge of his nose, he knew what the only explanation could be. Tony had not taken advantage of Lilli that night she'd been drugged. Some other man—some perverted stranger—had violated her. The only consolation he could find was that at least Lilli had no memory of the event.

He thought of little David and felt a surge of protectiveness. The baby *was* his. In every way that mattered. That child had burrowed into Max's heart so deeply he'd never be able to extricate him. Nor would he ever want to.

And Lilli. Max took a deep breath.

They'd made irrevocable vows to one another. He'd sworn to care for David as if he were his own. Now that the harsh emotions of the moment had passed, he knew he needed to go to her again. This time, he *would* listen.

After Lilli brought David back from his stroll, she rocked him for a long time. His soft warm body and sweetness were the only thing that reminded her she was alive. Setting him into his crib, she bent over to kiss his forehead and stared at him for a long while.

Softly closing the door to the nursery, she walked downstairs. Halfway down the steps, she heard a sound and saw Max standing just inside the front door. Her breath just stopped. She stared at him for a full moment, wondering if he was real.

"We need to talk," he said.

Her heart squeezing tight with dread, she followed him out onto the patio. The sunny afternoon provided a stark contrast to the desperation she felt inside her. She swallowed over a lump in her throat. "I understand if you want David and me to leave. I don't expect your support, especially now."

He held up his hand. "Lilli, I'm sorry I jumped to so many conclusions. I can guess what happened."

She closed her eyes. She couldn't look at him as she

recalled that terrible night she'd tried to forget. "Like I told you before, I told Tony I wanted to leave that night. He begged me to stay for just one more song, one more drink. I ordered a soda. I remember feeling dizzy, then nothing...until I woke up hours later in the back room of the club. I could tell something had happened," she said in a halting voice. "Tony was passed out next to the door. I couldn't get out of there fast enough. I got home and sat under the shower until the water turned cold." Opening her eyes, she shook her head, her tight throat reducing her voice to a whisper. "I'm so sorry, Max, but I swear I didn't know. I don't remember anything. And now there's this image of a faceless monster—"

"That's enough." He moved toward her and wrapped his arms around her. "No more," he said. "You've been through enough."

Lilli was afraid to believe her ears. Yet his strength surrounded her. His warmth, the scent she knew and loved. Could it be real?

Swiping at her tears, she cautiously searched his face. What she saw there almost made her knees buckle in relief. He believed her. She could see it clear as the sunlight. "You believe me, don't you?"

He nodded. "Yes, I do. I should have given you a chance to explain, but—"

She sniffed. "You thought you were looking after your brother's child and—" She lifted her shoulders. "And you're not." She took a deep breath and tried to steady herself. "If you want David and me to leave, we will."

"No," he said, the word as hard as steel. "I want you and David to stay. You two belong to me."

Lilli felt a surge of relief, but had to make sure. "But

won't you resent us? Won't you feel as if we're a burden that's been pushed on you?"

He shook his head. "I chose to marry you. I chose to adopt David. None of that has changed." He paused, slicing his hand through his hair. "The only thing that has changed is that now I know how vital you are to me, to my life. I never thought this would happen to me, but I love you. I don't want to live without you. Either of you."

Lilli felt as if the room turned upside down and this time her knees did buckle. Max caught her against him, sank into a chair and pulled her onto his lap. She lifted her trembling hands to his hard, but precious face. "I thought I was going to be all alone in my feelings. Loving you, but never having your love."

"But you married me anyway."

"How could I not? If there was a chance that I could make your life happier by being in it, then I wanted to be there for you. I love you so much."

He closed his eyes and shook his head as if he was overcome with emotion. "I kept saying I didn't understand how Tony could have been so damn lucky to find you. But I'm the lucky one. I get to keep you. Forever," he said, sealing the words with a kiss.

"Forever," she echoed, "But I'm the lucky one. I got the man of steel who has a heart of gold."

* * * * *

Look for the next book in Leanne Banks's series
THE BILLIONAIRE CLUB
this August from Silhouette Desire

Look for LAST WOLF WATCHING
by Rhyannon Byrd—the exciting conclusion in the
BLOODRUNNERS miniseries
from Silhouette Nocturne.

Follow Michaela and Brody on their fierce journey to
find the truth and face the demons from the past,
as they reach the heart of the battle between the
Runners and the rogues.

Here is a sneak preview of book three,
LAST WOLF WATCHING.

Michaela squinted, struggling to see through the impenetrable darkness. Everyone looked toward the Elders, but she knew Brody Carter still watched her. Michaela could feel the power of his gaze. Its heat. Its strength. And something that felt strangely like anger, though he had no reason to have any emotion toward her. Strangers from different worlds, brought together beneath the heavy silver moon on a night made for hell itself. That was their only connection.

The second she finished that thought, she knew it was a lie. But she couldn't deal with it now. Not tonight. Not when her whole world balanced on the edge of destruction.

Willing her backbone to keep her upright, Michaela Doucet focused on the towering blaze of a roaring bonfire that rose from the far side of the clearing, its orange flames burning with maniacal zeal against the inky black curtain of the night. Many of the Lycans had already shifted into their preternatural shapes, their fur-covered bodies standing like monstrous shadows at the edges of the forest as they waited with restless expectancy for her brother.

Her nineteen-year-old brother, Max, had been attacked by a rogue werewolf—a Lycan who preyed upon humans for food. Max had been bitten in the attack, which meant he was no longer human, but a breed of creature that existed between the two worlds of man and beast, much like the Bloodrunners themselves.

The Elders parted, and two hulking shapes emerged from the trees. In their wolf forms, the Lycans stood over seven feet tall, their legs bent at an odd angle as they stalked forward. They each held a thick chain that had been wound around their inside wrists, the twin lengths leading back into the shadows. The Lycans had taken no more than a few steps when they jerked on the chains, and her brother appeared.

Bound like an animal.

Biting at her trembling lower lip, she glanced left, then right, surprised to see that others had joined her. Now the Bloodrunners and their family and friends stood as a united force against the Silvercrest pack, which had yet to accept the fact that something sinister was eating away at its foundation—something that would rip down the protective walls that separated their world from the humans'. It occurred to Michaela that loyalties were being announced tonight—a separation made between those who would stand with the Runners in their fight against the rogues and those who blindly supported the pack's refusal to face reality. But all she could focus on was her brother. Max looked so hurt…so terrified.

"Leave him alone," she screamed, her soft-soled, black satin slip-ons struggling for purchase in the damp earth as she rushed toward Max, only to find herself lifted off the ground when a hard, heavily muscled arm clamped around her waist from behind, pulling her clear off her feet. "Damn it, let me down!" she snarled, unable to take her eyes off her brother as the golden-eyed Lycan kicked him.

Mindless with heartache and rage, Michaela clawed at the arm holding her, kicking her heels against whatever part of her captor's legs she could reach. "Stop it," a deep, husky voice grunted in her ear. "You're not helping him by losing it. I give you my word he'll survive the ceremony, but you have to keep it together."

"Nooooo!" she screamed, too hysterical to listen to reason. "You're monsters! All of you! Look what you've done to him! How dare you! *How dare you!*"

The arm tightened with a powerful flex of muscle, cinching her waist. Her breath sucked in on a sharp, wailing gasp.

"Shut up before you get both yourself and your brother killed. I will *not* let that happen. Do you understand me?" her captor growled, shaking her so hard that her teeth clicked together. "Do you understand me, Doucet?"

"Damn it," she cried, stricken as she watched one of the guards grab Max by his hair. Around them Lycans huffed and growled as they watched the spectacle, while others outright howled for the show to begin.

"That's enough!" the voice seethed in her ear. "They'll tear you apart before you even reach him, and I'll be damned if I'm going to stand here and watch you die."

Suddenly, through the haze of fear and agony and outrage in her mind, she finally recognized who'd caught her. *Brody.*

He held her in his arms, her body locked against his powerful form, her back to the burning heat of his chest. A low, keening sound of anguish tore through her, and her head dropped forward as hoarse sobs of pain ripped from her throat. "Let me go. I have to help him. *Please,*" she begged brokenly, knowing only that she needed to get to Max. "Let me go, Brody."

He muttered something against her hair, his breath warm against her scalp, and Michaela could have sworn it was a single word…. But she must have heard wrong. She was too upset. Too furious. Too terrified. She must be out of her mind.

Because it sounded as if he'd quietly snarled the word *never.*

HARLEQUIN® *Romance*®

Western Weddings

Jason Welborn was convinced that his business
partner's daughter, Jenny, had come to claim her share
in the business. But Jenny seemed determined to win
him over, and the more he tried to push her away, the
more feisty Jenny's response. Slowly but surely she
was starting to get under Jason's skin....

Look for

Coming Home to the Cattleman

by

JUDY CHRISTENBERRY

Available May wherever you buy books.

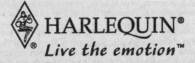

REQUEST YOUR FREE BOOKS!

2 FREE NOVELS PLUS 2 FREE GIFTS!

Silhouette® Desire®

Passionate, Powerful, Provocative!

YES! Please send me 2 FREE Silhouette Desire® novels and my 2 FREE gifts (gifts are worth about $10). After receiving them, if I don't wish to receive any more books, I can return the shipping statement marked "cancel". If I don't cancel, I will receive 6 brand-new novels every month and be billed just $4.05 per book in the U.S. or $4.74 per book in Canada, plus 25¢ shipping and handling per book and applicable taxes, if any*. That's a savings of almost 15% off the cover price! I understand that accepting the 2 free books and gifts places me under no obligation to buy anything. I can always return a shipment and cancel at any time. Even if I never buy another book, the two free books and gifts are mine to keep forever.

225 SDN ERVX 326 SDN ERVM

Name	(PLEASE PRINT)
Address	Apt. #
City	State/Prov.
	Zip/Postal Code

Signature (if under 18, a parent or guardian must sign)

Mail to the Silhouette Reader Service:
IN U.S.A.: P.O. Box 1867, Buffalo, NY 14240-1867
IN CANADA: P.O. Box 609, Fort Erie, Ontario L2A 5X3

Not valid to current subscribers of Silhouette Desire books.

Want to try two free books from another line?
Call 1-800-873-8635 or visit www.morefreebooks.com.

* Terms and prices subject to change without notice. N.Y. residents add applicable sales tax. Canadian residents will be charged applicable provincial taxes and GST. This offer is limited to one order per household. All orders subject to approval. Credit or debit balances in a customer's account(s) may be offset by any other outstanding balance owed by or to the customer. Please allow 4 to 6 weeks for delivery. Offer available while quantities last.

Your Privacy: Silhouette Books is committed to protecting your privacy. Our Privacy Policy is available online at www.eHarlequin.com or upon request from the Reader Service. From time to time we make our lists of customers available to reputable third parties who may have a product or service of interest to you. If you would prefer we not share your name and address, please check here. ☐

SDES08

SILHOUETTE

SPECIAL EDITION™

THE WILDER FAMILY
Healing Hearts in Walnut River

Social worker Isobel Suarez was proud to
work at Walnut River General Hospital, so
when Neil Kane showed up from the attorney
general's office to investigate insurance fraud,
she was up in arms. Until she melted in his
arms, and things got very tricky...

Look for

HER MR. RIGHT?

by

KAREN ROSE SMITH

Available May wherever books are sold.

COMING NEXT MONTH

#1867 BOARDROOMS & A BILLIONAIRE HEIR—
Paula Roe
Diamonds Down Under

She'd been blackmailed into spying on Sydney's most infamous corporate raider. Until he turned the tables and seduced her into a marriage of convenience.

#1868 FALLING FOR KING'S FORTUNE—Maureen Child
Kings of California

This millionaire playboy was about to enter a loveless marriage sure to make his wallet bigger...until a woman he'd never met claimed to be the mother of his child.

#1869 MISTRESS FOR A MONTH—Ann Major

He will stop at nothing to get her inheritance. But her price is for her to become his mistress...for a month.

#1870 DANTE'S STOLEN WIFE—Day Leclaire
The Dante Legacy

The curse of *The Inferno* left this billionaire determined to make her his bride...and he doesn't care that she's his own twin brother's fiancée.

#1871 SHATTERED BY THE CEO—Emilie Rose
The Payback Affairs

To fulfill the terms of his father's will, a business tycoon must convince his former love to work for his company—and try to find a way to stay out of her bed.

#1872 THE DESERT LORD'S BABY—Olivia Gates
Throne of Judar

He must marry and produce an heir if he is to become king. But he doesn't know his ex-lover has already given birth to his child....